DEATH OR GLORY

SIR PATRICK BIJOU

PRELUDE

Hell had broken into the Universe.

There was simply no other way to describe what happened.

Simultaneously, every planet boasting sentient life forms was attacked. It came without warning, and no seers could have predicted the outcome either.

The day had started like any other until portals began to rip through time and space, and demons of unimaginable horror poured through, destroying everything in their paths.

Peaceful cities were torn down, families were separated, and great sacrifices were made — no amount of heroism could've saved the Universe anymore.

After all, there were absolutely no survivors left.

This was why it was no wonder that when 18 pairs of eyes opened to an unfamiliar world, they were only filled with fear and confusion. Looking around, they cautiously watched each other. Their surroundings were terrified that the demons would jump out when they were unguarded.

"Are... are we dead?"

They weren't — not for long, at least.

Get transported to an insane world where fighting for survival is your only option. You'll never know if the person beside you is a friend or foe in this fast-paced, action-filled fantasy story where absolutely anything could happen at any moment. With a colourful cast from different backgrounds and strange voices emanating from orbs, this adventure will surely keep you on the edge of your seat.

Safety is a luxury that our cast simply cannot afford. **Welcome to a place where it's either Death...** *or Glory.*

ABOUT THE AUTHOR

Sir Patrick Bijou lives and writes from the United Kingdom and is the author of several books on finance and fiction. He is known for his extraordinary skills in settling and negotiating peace settlements and international law and is a prodigious legal and political adviser. His diverse writing ability has been influenced by many experiences, making him the success he is today.

Sir Patrick has written many books and articles about the liberation of people, highlighting the issues of those whom the literary world of creative writing has not enlightened. His expedition into content writing has made him a remarkably inspired author and professional communicator.

He has written over 40 non-fictional and fictional books spanning different genres.

Finding his Books.

To find out more about Sir Patrick, visit his website.

www.sirpatrickbijou.com

www.bijouebook.com

TABLE OF CONTENTS

CHAPTER 1

Hell. It was the only word really to describe what occurred—unbridled, unexpected hell. Throughout the Universe, on every planet boasting sentient life forms, the attack occurred simultaneously and without warning. Portals opened, and great demons of unimaginable strength and power flooded through, destroying everything in their path. There were some, of course, who fought. Some made great sacrifices, and others exacted amazing feats of heroism to stop the invaders, but in the end, no one survived.

This was why those who awoke in the strange world were initially disoriented. Of course, they had believed they had died, and this was, in fact, the truth. In the final breath of each person who awoke in the circle in the glade, a realization of their fate had become all too real. Death had been upon them, and they would soon be with their maker.

Confused and disoriented eyes blinked as rivulets of pure sunlight spackled across their faces. There were 18 people in total, and they were all resting on the soft grass, their bodies arranged so that they formed a circle around a central blue orb that hovered passively before their feet. Among the 18 were nine men and nine women, all appearing from different portions of their world.

Certainly, few recognized the styles of the garments of the others. The unfamiliarity of their mutual companions only served to further the confusion. As they awoke, some responded by dashing instantly to their feet, quickly eyeing their surroundings as if prepared for a demon to jump out at any moment.

Others were more cautious in their movements. Nearly all of them wore the undergarments to plate or other armor, and while their garments were clean, it was what they had been wearing when they had died. Those cautious seemed to make this discovery first, noting that their armor and weapons had been removed, leaving them with only their persons for company.

Though the circle had no direction of preference, there was among them a young woman clad in a strange but lovely dress. She couldn't have been more than her late twenties in age, and unlike many of the others, the woman continued to lay in her spot. Her eyes glazed upward to the sky as though she weren't certain it was real. Eventually, she raised a hand upward, and then, upon catching sight of her hand, she began to search over her arm and hand, seemingly very interested, if not surprised, to see it.

Very slowly, the young woman sat up, still studying the integrity of her body. Her hands ran over her head and then pushed through long brown locks, again very surprised to have made the discovery.

If nothing else, while she registered that there were others around her, she seemed wildly uninterested in anyone else, presuming they didn't get too close.

Unlike many others, who were dressed in various degrees of armor, the woman was wearing a rather elegant gown. The gown style certainly did not seem like anything traditional, but there were many lands and cultures, and who knew what nobles in other parts would wear?

"Are... Are we dead?" Asked a young man immediately to her right. He wore a simple grey tunic and seemed disappointed as if he had expected more to cover it. The question was innocent and raw, and the noblewoman to his left seemed to register that words had been spoken.

She almost gasped at the terror of the surprise, apparently only just now realizing that others were there. Her grey-green eyes scanned the rest of the circle, taking in each new face like a cornered cat assessing an opponent with wild eyes.

"I was about to ask the same myself," replied an elderly man to the young man's right. Unlike those more youthful, he seemed to have difficulty propping himself up with such ease. "Is this place familiar to you... friend?" He inquired in a friendly tone, unsure how to address the young man who spoke.

"R-Robin. Robin Tenderfoot," the younger man answered as if not totally sure of himself. Robin, like the noblewoman, couldn't have been older than 30. His hair was cut short, save for a small braided lock at the nape of his neck and his eyes were a mix of silver and green. "I am a cleric of the honorable Heironeous," he added, this time with more surity.

"I have seen many places, but this is unfamiliar to me...?" The statement trailed into a question as Robin hoped the man would similarly introduce himself.

"Albus Zediferous," the older man replied with the sort of smile only age could season. "I am familiar with Heironeous," he added, seeming to be more at ease by the introduction. "Delleb bids his followers to cooperate with your following. The pleasure is mine, good priest."

As the two hesitantly made their exchanges, others took note. A rather handsome man with defined features slowly pushed himself up. At first, he made to defend himself from an unseen foe, but when an attack never transpired, he stared in a bewildered haze around him. The transition between such violence and peace was profound and left many reeling from the emotions.

Though the man heard the exchange, his eyes shifted to the noblewoman to his right. If he had read her expression well enough, and he usually did, she was not at all familiar with Delleb or Heironeous, only furthering her confusion. That seemed intriguing to him, but it was not pronounced enough to capture his attention at the moment.

"My Lady, pardon my... forgive me bold demeanor; but could you tell me? Is this the Seven Heavens, home to Rao and the place of judgment for our souls in the afterlife?" he spoke roughly at first, his tone seeming to smooth as if he remembered a manner forgotten initially but recalled as if he was born to it.

The woman did not seem to pay much attention to the questions, and the more she examined herself, the more emotionally distraught she became, though not to the point of histrionics. The only evidence she lent to her internal turmoil was a mild glassiness to her eyes and her chest's rapid rising and falling as she struggled to keep calm. She looked like someone who did not believe that what she was experiencing was real; It was a look that marked a contrast. Where ever she had been prior to waking in this paradise (by comparison), it was a stark enough difference to prompt the psychological response of denial.

It was only when the apparent nobleman spoke to her that her gaze finally fixed on something other than her own physical integrity. Her bright grey-green eyes flickered up to the deep green of the nobleman, settling upon him a gaze so intense and filled with such a commanding presence that most would be compelled to look away.

She said nothing, and yet, multitudes. The expression embodied the very confusion and hesitation felt by all the others. The woman opened her mouth to answer, unsure of herself and hesitant, and it was in that pause that others started to stir and speak as well. Several women stood together, all seeming curious about the orb at the circle's center.

"What tha fook are ya talk'n 'bout?" Came a rather lyrical voice from a man dressed in attire that seemed foreign to almost everyone there. "Thar ain't but one heaven. An' ain't ther suppose' ta be a pearly gate or some such? Saint Peter and all da angels?" The man's brow frowned from confusion as he responded to the rather handsome man on behalf of the noblewoman.

The young noblewoman turned to look at the man as he spoke, her eyes watching his mannerisms with keen discernment as though she were studying him like a specimen.

Before anyone could speak further, the blue orb erupted into a pure white light that shot up into the heavens. Those who had gathered near it gasped and recoiled with the surprise. The orb did not seem malicious. In fact, it had a feel to it that was rather comforting, though no one had stopped to consider this.

"Greetings, our beloved," a tranquil voice boomed from the light that now flooded the area. "Do not be afraid, for a great gift has been bestowed upon you. The battle has ended, but not all has been lost. Collected from among our faithful, you represent the future, our beloved. You have been taken from a place of evil and death and brought to a world of perfection. Here you will receive the reward you have earned for your valiant efforts to save that which was tainted. Here you will give life to a world untouched by evil. Here you will find salvation."

"Live in peace, our beloved, and be fruitful so that blessed goodness can reign freely and without fear. Beyond this glade is a city that is built for you. All you could require is provided, and we have designed a home for each. Live in peace, our beloved, and make this place a world of goodness untouched by evil. Live in peace."

As quickly as the orb had released the warm, white light, it ceased, falling lifeless to the ground.

Momentarily, the people were too stunned to speak, staring in awe at the now motionless orb that had dropped carelessly to the grass.

Wide eyes slowly started to connect as everyone began searching for answers among everyone else. The noblewoman's eyes rested on a man who wore a simple black robe with a white rectangle affixed on the throat of his collar. Understanding swept over her features, and she darted to her feet in an instant, only to collapse at his. "F- father?" She inquired, much to the interest of the others there. They hadn't recognized anyone, and learning that family members were present was intriguing.

The man with the strange, fey-like accent had a similar expression, and he also walked over to the pair. "Fater," the man said reverently. "Are we... Is this heaven, fater?"

As the three apparent family members began speaking softly to one another, the handsome man turned his attention to Robin. His expression was painted with confusion and tinges of hope. "You are a cleric of Heronious," he commented softly as means of a segway into an introduction. "I am Istvan, loyal servant of Rao. It pains me to ask... you seem as one who would have the knowledge to share with others. Please, good sir. What do you make of this?"

"I don't know what to think," the man answered. "I am Robin," he added, extending his hand toward Istvan's to help him to his feet. Several people were already heading toward the aforementioned village, and Robin made for walking that way, with Istvan following uncertainly.

Robin frowned slightly. "I believe our answers will be in the village, Istvan. It is not in the nature of Heironeous to be dishonest, so I must believe that we all were placed here for the purpose that he expressed; salvation. The battle against the demons certainly was not boding well," he added with a sense of humiliation.

There was a brief pause. "I believe our first action after investigating this village will be to ensure the women are safe. This could be a deception by the demons, and I shall not dishonor my lord with further failure."

"I certainly hope I am not one of these women to which you are referring," commented a woman whose stature indicated she was a fighter of some sort. "You will learn swiftly, Robin, servant of Heironeous, that not all women need to be rescued or protected."

Robin's expression remained unchanged and discerning. "And you would be, miss?"

"I am a servant of the most esteemed St Cuthbert, Heironite," she answered sternly.

"Yes, I can see that by the symbol you boast," Robin continued gently. "I was asking for your name."

"Tracy," she answered flatly as she increased her pace to get out of range and pass the pair.

Robin let out a small sigh but said nothing. They would be in the village within a few more steps, and he would have his answers. Istvan looked back at what he assumed was a family reunion, feeling comforted by it.

Istvan turned back and offered Robin as much of a reassuring smile as he could. "Yes," he replied, "That is most chivalrous. I shall, of course, aid you were I can, good priest, but I was never much of a fighter," he commented as his eyes drifted over to a man of massive proportions. Istvan didn't even bother questioning his assessment; he was likely the most stereotypical barbarian he had ever seen. His stature alone was enough to cause concern in almost everyone, particularly since all their weapons had been removed.

"That is apparent," commented a man from behind him. Like Tracy, this man proudly wore the symbol of St. Cuthbert, pushing past Robin and Istvan to catch up with the apparent Paladin.

Istvan frowned and was prepared to retort to the rather rude man when Robin spoke to him, distracting him back to their previous conversation. "It pleases me that you feel similarly, Istvan," Robin replied, also eying the barbarian with distrust. "For our own concerns... others will be comforted by our care toward the weaker sex. I believe it will be important to establish order quickly as we investigate the nature of our presence here. Ah. There is a chapel with a bell in its steeple as well." Robin let out a relieved sigh, offering Istvan a hopeful grin.

"Perhaps we should join the others in search of the village? Once we have neared completion, I shall ring the bell and summon a gathering so that we may discuss together what is to happen to us in this place." Robin clasped his hand on Istvan's shoulder before trotting off to investigate the village.

The men walked into the village square. The place was extremely clean and well-ordered as if it had never been used. A few shops and a look inside proved that they were well stocked and ready for the inhabitants. In fact, many of the others were already loitering around inside various edifices. Further down the road was the chapel, which stood in the center of the town. To its right was a building with a sign displaying a scroll and a book. Istvan did not have to guess; it was a library. It was here that Robin moved off on his own to do some more exploring, permitting Istvan an extended look inside.

The older man who had introduced himself as Albus was not far behind them, also heading for the library. Istvan was curious but always a dignified and polite man. "Greetings," he offered in a friendly enough voice. "I see I do not search the library alone. I am Istvan, friend," he continued.

"Albus," the man replied with a polite smile. "And it is always a pleasure to meet those who delight in knowledge."

Istvan's smile broadened more genuinely. "I am a devotee of Rao," he replied. "I would be amiss not to avail myself to the library, particularly if a follower of Delleb is present. I can only imagine the knowledge you must hold."

"Ah, Rao? The god of the community!" The older man replied. "Then it is a pleasure, indeed."

Without further coaxing, both men walked inside the building, heading directly for the nearest stack of books. Each one they pulled, however, revealed nothing but blank pages.

Book after book, it was the same. The books were all empty. Albus frowned and turned to Istvan, who exchanged a similar expression. "Why would one go to the trouble of compiling a library of empty books?" The older man asked rhetorically.

"... Perhaps we are meant to fill them?" Istvan returned pensively. He didn't know himself, but the suggestion was not unreasonable. Istvan paused, taking in the older man. "Forgive me if I am presumptuous, but you have the look of a mage to you, whiskers and all," he approached delicately. "Is this true?"

Albus offered a kind and pleasantly surprised smile. "Yes," he answered. "I indeed study the Arcane, though..." the man's voice trailed slightly. "In my land, the Cuthbertians have made the Arcane a target. I do not make a habit of announcing as much..."

Istvan waived the man's concern away. "I understand," he answered with a grin. "I shall not comment on it. In truth, our occupations are similar. I am an artificer, and it would bring me great joy to engage your mind in the arcane were you compelled... I do not suppose you-"

Istvan was interrupted by the sound of two people talking.

"Nah, Maddy, what are ya goin' in there for?" Came the voice of the man with the fey-like accent.

"It's a library," the noblewoman answered as though this were obvious.

"Yea? So?" He asked.

"I want to see if any books in there can tell me what's going on," she tiredly answered. "If you don't want to come, Father went to check out that chapel... thing."

The man scoffed. "You think I'm going to let you wander'n about with all these freaks? You're out of your fooking mind, lass."

"John, you don't even-" the woman cut off what she was going to say as she entered the library to see Istvan and Albus already going through the shelves. "E-excuse me," she offered quietly to the pair as she averted her vision to avoid eye contact. The noblewoman and the younger man had walked up to her and her father.

Like Istvan, and presumably Albus before him, the woman named Maddy moved toward one of the bookshelves and pulled out a book, frowning deeply upon discovering it was blank. She replaced the book and took out another to make the same discovery.

"What's the matter?" John asked her.

"They're blank," she answered.

"They are all blank," Albus told her gently. "So far, that is."

"Have you checked them all?" She asked, genuinely concerned. Her eyes met Albus's, and he took a sharp breath. She only had to make eye contact to intimidate; this was unintentional. Albus let his breath out and smiled sadly, shaking his head.

John let out a sigh while crossing his arms across his chest. "Come on now, lass. Let's get back to him. Ain't no answers in here."

As quickly as they had arrived, Maddy and John turned to leave. Istvan, however, was far too curious about them and set down his book, moving quickly over to the pair. "Excuse me, miss sir," he addressed them in a gentle voice. "Forgive me, but I could not help but hear that your family was brought here together."

The woman's eyes widened slightly. "... What?" She inquired out of impressed confusion. "W- where? How did you know they were my family?" There was an innocent hope in her voice that showed Istvan with heartbreaking accuracy that there had been some misunderstanding.

"Y-your father?" He replied, quickly realizing that the man was likely not her birth father. "I-... I am sorry. I assumed the man to be-"

"You're kidding, right?" The man named John interrupted with a scoff. "She ain't me sister, nor are we related to the Fater. He's a priest. Father Anthony. He ain't me, pa. Come on, Maddy, let's get goin'."

Maddy lingered for a moment, casting a very subtle look of apology to Istvan and Albus. At that moment, Istvan's frown deepened. Only a fool would have missed her swell with hope only to be thrown down to the ground again. The woman blinked a few times, returning her gaze to John.

The noblewoman gave John a hard look at his demand that they leave the library. Like Istvan and Albus, she hadn't even begun to explore the bookshelves. The woman did not strike either of them as weak, though she did have a distant expression on her face as if she wasn't interested in arguing. "I can see the church from the window," she replied with an arched eyebrow. She did not take orders from John, and this seemed obvious to everyone but John.

"An? Wha's yar point, lass?" He replied, folding his arms across his chest and looking at her seriously. "Look, I don't think it's a good idea ta separate right now..."

The arched eyebrow took on an even greater look of skepticism before resolving to apathy. "Whatever..." she let out a sigh as she put the book back and half-heartedly followed him out the door toward the Chapel. Their father had gone there first, and it wasn't until Istvan and Albus heard the church bell sounding that they decided to join the others.

What they saw, however, was not expected. Robin had a wide-eyed look of terror, while Tracy and the other Cuthbertian had stone-faced seriousness. The man tossed the Father of the two strange individuals to the ground, and the man rolled to his back, a look of terror that mirrored Robin's on his face.

"What is the meaning of this?" Demanded a dark-skinned clericess. Her fists had clenched, and others were standing behind her with a similar demeanor of resolution.

Meanwhile, the noblewoman rushed toward the fallen man to attempt to help him up and get him out the danger.

"Please, m'Lady," announced Robin gently as he moved toward her, "Please step away. This man is not what he seems."

"Ya have about five seconds to explain before I start crack'n skulls," John replied violently.

Tracy cocked an eyebrow at John skeptically as she tossed a leather-bound book into the ground next to the man. "His holy book is written in Infernal. He was speaking it."

The noblewoman said nothing, but as her eyes found the book, her entire emotional state was displayed. It was as if relief and disbelief flooded over her all at once. "Where did you find this?" She asked, the awe betrayed by her tone. "They burned them all." Her hand hovered over the book with deep reverence.

The other Cuthbertian cocked his eyebrow at her reaction, but Tracy reacted by reaching down to yank Madeline up by her arm. "You subscribe to this as well?" She inquired firmly.

The icy and powerful look Maddy cast Tracy was something the female paladin was utterly unprepared to receive. She was so shocked that her hand loosened on Maddy's arm and the smaller woman yanked herself free with precise action. "Don't ever touch me again," she almost growled in a tone that emulated the powerful look. When Maddy wanted to intimidate, it was guaranteed.

The dark-skinned cleric now looked unsure of who to attack. "Infernal is the tongue of devils," she explained seriously. "Is this true? You worship devils?"

"What? Are you fook'n insane?" John retorted, now positioning himself between the soldiers and the prone priest. He was starting to panic. The other group had them flanked. The only one who didn't look concerned was Maddy. If anything, she looked apathetic. "We worship gad ya fool. Gad hates the devil..."

"Please," begged their father. "There is some misunderstanding. We do not worship the devil; we worship the one true god. I was praying in Latin, the tongue of the church. I assure you; we mean no harm."

"I wouldn't say that father," John replied firmly. "They touch ya again, and they'll see the harm they won't forget."

"Little man, no touch, cleric," boomed the voice of the barbarian man. "Thorn, kill the devil. Thorn kill devil worship."

"Bring it on, ya big footer," John hissed, now turning to face the most obvious threat.

"Enough!" shouted the dark-skinned clericess, whose expression was solidly threatening in her own right. Several other women stepped up behind her, one of which seemed strong enough to take John up on his retort without a weapon.

Chaos broke out at that moment. The enormous Barbarian leaped forward at John, who dove out of the way with seasoned ease.

"STOP THIS!" Shouted Istvan over the chaos, stepping forward as Maddy stooped again, attempting to collect the priest from the ground as quickly as possible. All three of the strange people had wide eyes and looked like they would run. "There must be an explanation! I heard the voice of Rao himself just an hour past. Have you all so quickly forgotten? We were placed here for peace; all of us!"

"You don't know that," replied an older woman behind him. "What if this is all some sort of trap? That evil is lowering our guard to better kill us?"

Albus squinted slightly. "Powerful enough to bring us to this place but foolish enough to place a book of devils in plain site?" The man inquired.

"There is a barrel in the chapel labeled Blood of Christ," The male Cuthbertian announced. "They drink blood and speak in the tongue of devils. What more evidence is necessary?"

"Wait," insisted Robin. "I insist they are permitted an opportunity to explain this evil."

"Father," Maddy insisted quickly. "Take the Bible and run," she said, grabbing the book and thrusting it into his hands. "Get it safe."

"I do not think that is wise," came the voice of another towering man with a thick dwarven accent as he stepped forward and pulled the priest up by his arm. He was firm but not violent. "There will be answers, little woman."

"Please," the man continued urgently as panic swelled in his voice. "Allow them to leave. They are innocent -"

The man was interrupted as John slammed his fists into the back of the dwarven-speaking man, sending him down to the ground in a groan. That instant, Thorn tackled the smaller man from behind. A battle for control ensued, one which the smaller man was unlikely to win, though much to everyone else's horror, it was a much more closely matched battle than expected. "RUN, MADDY!" He bellowed at the noblewoman, who was already starting to back away.

Istvan couldn't allow this to continue. In a swift move, his arm shot out and latched onto the woman's, eliciting the same powerful glare and recoil that the paladiness had experienced. Much to the surprise of others, the father of two stopped and checked on the dwarven-speaking man rather than running away. "No, please!" He pleaded with the others. "I submit freely. There is no need for this violence! Please stop this. This man needs medical attention!"

The Cuthbertian sneered at them as, finally, the barbarian could restrain the man named John. "Come and see the evidence yourself," he stated impassively. "I certainly am curious for an explanation for this apparent trickery," He cast a skeptical glance toward Robin. "I trust this is just in our approach?" The sarcasm was obvious in his tone.

Istvan sighed heavily as he directed the woman to move forward. It wasn't ideal, but for the moment, it was keeping blood from being shed, and it would allow them to explain themselves in a less violent setting. The woman's jaw tensed, and her arm flexed under his grip. "Let me go this second," she stated firmly. "I swear to god I will kill anyone who touches that man, you understand?" She was talking about the priest willingly walking toward the temple, though, had John not been in such a violent battle for freedom; he'd have swelled slightly in pride at her disposition.

Istvan frowned at her. He didn't release her but wasn't forceful either. "No one will hurt him," he answered her patiently. "You have my word; you will not be harmed, m'Lady -"

"I don't give a fuck about me," she answered sharply. "If you idiots harm a hair on his head, I will destroy you." The seriousness of her voice was not easily mistaken, and Istvan tensed. He was glad they were only a few steps from the church.

The Cuthbertians led the way, indicating what appeared to be a closet where they could lock John for the time being. So long as the other two complied, they were more or less free to move. John fought the imprisonment with everything he had, taking four men to get him inside and then barring the door. Even after being confined, his fierce battle did not subside, and he beat the door violently, threatening to break it off the hinges.

At this point, Maddy began resisting Istvan's grip on her arms. "Do you have any idea who he is?" She demanded in a fury. Istvan could easily restrain her, but he was impressed with her strength for her size nonetheless. "What the hell is wrong with you people?"

Robin ran his trembling hand through his hair as he sighed deeply. "This is not ideal," he commented to himself. He looked up at the two in question, which remained, Maddy, looking like she would rip off someone's head, and the priest, looking mostly bewildered and concerned on John's behalf. The others appeared a range of bewildered, furious, and terrified. "My name is Robin Tenderfoot," he announced to everyone. "I am a cleric of Heironeous from the Gran Marsh. As such, I would hope you take this to understand my desire for Justice. No harm will befall these Three, even if we learn them to be agents of the devils..." He sighed deeply as he sat heavily on one of the pews. The noblewoman's nose wrinkled in further confusion. Apparently, she had not heard of Heironeous to gain any comfort from the proclamation. About a quarter of those there seemed confused. However, the others did seem to make the connection and gave Robin the desired effect. "I had been hoping we could discuss what we could do to learn more about what has happened to us and how we have come here, not begin this new world with a trial..."

"What has happened to us?" A very beautiful woman asked incredulously. "We died. That is what happened to us."

"Well... well, I suppose, but... well, that is not what I meant, miss," Robin answered, clearly unsure of himself.

"I believe the young man is correct," Albus announced. "It would behoove us to understand this situation better, particularly to put any questions of evil to rest here. As Istvan said earlier, did we not just see the Gods themselves? I witnessed the most holy Delleb. Such is not an event to take in passing. I am something of a scholar to my people. My name is Albus Zediphorus. I would be happy to assist in this matter."

"As would I," Istvan concurred through a tired sigh. "If we are mistaken, we have alienated three of our own with this misunderstanding. This does not benefit any community... I am Istvan Caracus from Sharn in Khorvaire. It would be my pleasure was this under better circumstances." He frowned when only the sage-like woman among them seemed to recognize the name of his home city. It was the largest in the world; surely others had heard of it?

"I am Lady Jacely of Brandobia, Queen of Brandobia," chimed in a sweet and articulate voice. "I agree with Mister Caracus and Mister Zediphorus. As a noble, I insist you handle this woman with deep respect, for if Mr. Caracus is correct and this is a misunderstanding, one of our future leaders will oppose us." Jacelyn was furious and was advocating for Maddy, her eyes shooting hot daggers into Istvan's hold on Maddy's arm.

The man blushed slightly, releasing Maddy and scratching the back of his neck in embarrassment. For her part, Maddy threw his hands off and promptly moved over to check on the priest. He was scratched and bruised, but there were no serious injuries.

The woman's jaw tightened, and she turned to address the others with a well-restrained fury that boiled under her skin. She would have been truly terrifying if she had been anything other than a lithe woman. Her eyes went first to those who had introduced themselves and then to others, but the priest next spoke first. "My name is Antonio Del Fonte," he said in his dragon-borne accent. "I am a Catholic Priest," he announced, hoping that would abate some of this tension. It didn't, only adding to his own personal concern. "This is Madeline Parker; she is an American... and the man you have locked away is John Reece from Ireland. They are also Catholic." Antonio had been counting on the others to recognize the name America or Catholic, and when no one did, he looked alarmed.

"They don't know what that means, father," Madeline told him firmly, though clearly with respect. She had winced when he introduced her, and her posture indicated that she expected to be attacked immediately. Her reply caused anxiety to swell within the man.

"They don't know who John is, even though they should." Her eyes locked on Robin's. "And we don't know who Heironeous is to trust that you understand what Justice means, Mr. Tenderfoot. Or Rao," she added, looking at Istvan, "Or Delleb," turning to look at Albus. "And we've never heard of Brandobia, Miss... Jacelyn." Madeline's eyebrows flickered slightly, clearly trying to figure out how to address Jacelyn without knowing her last name. Jacelyn flinched at the lack of a proper title but said nothing.

"Perhaps not," intoned the male Cuthbertian in an oily smooth voice, "But we are quite familiar with Infernal." That seemed to be unanimously agreed upon. "And no holy book in all planes has ever been penned in such an offensive text. Fear not. Mine is the God of Inquisition, and the truth will be uncovered. I am Sir Simon of Trent, Archduke of Onara, a loyal follower of Saint Cuthbert, and skilled in inquiry. Lady Tracy Quickfeather, a paladin of the noblest Saint Cuthbert, is equally qualified." The paladinness nodded once.

Madeline's face contorted into skepticism. Antonio stepped forward as the woman opened her mouth, prepared to elaborate on her confusion. Antonio was equally confused, but he was the clear diplomat of the two of them. "Excellent," he replied, attempting to meet these strange people halfway. "We also relish in the truth. Ours is the god of love, but one cannot have truth without love. You will find us most accommodating to the truth and desiring peace." Madeline offered him a skeptical look, particularly as the tirade of John continued in the background.

The dark-skinned clericess seemed to relax considerably. "I am Natalia Romanofski, Grand Priestess of Sarenrae over all of Glorious," she announced as though this should mean something important and revealing. To her surprise, only one person there seemed to know what this meant. "If yours is the god of Love, why is your book written in the tongue of devils?" She knew full well that the God of Love did not use such a language.

Madeline folded her arms across her chest, seemingly now convinced that no one would try to kill her outright. Letting out an impatient sigh, she stepped backward and sat in a pew, clearly content with allowing Antonio to answer on their behalf. Antonio forced a confident smile, trying to reclaim his endlessly patient demeanor. Internally, his heart was pounding furiously in his chest. He knew if he could explain, he could probably diffuse the situation, but the level of confusion was alarming nonetheless.

"The book is written in Latin," he offered gently. "It is not the language of our god; it was the language of the era and region where our faith could blossom, and so our texts were written in it and Greek, another regional language. Latin is no longer spoken; it is an ancient, archaic language. While I do not doubt that the devil knows how to speak it, I am certain he can speak any tongue we humans use."

This explanation did not go a long way with most people there, and Antonio swallowed slightly. "The language is dead. It's just a tool," he said, starting on another approach. "We use it in the church because it will not change with popular use so that the meanings of our holy texts are not lost with time... surely you have similar tools?"

Robin stepped forward and brought his hands to his temples in frustration. "The more I learn, the more confused I become. Your explanation for why your holy text is written in Infernal could make sense, but it does not explain the vat of blood. My heart tells me you are not evil, but -"

"But the facts point to the contrary," Tracy interrupted with an arched eyebrow.

Madeline rolled her eyes. "Facts? So far, all you've provided is ignorance. Let me know when these facts of yours surface..." Tracy's eyes narrowed though she did not advance on the smaller woman, who was not intimidated.

Antonio was growing frustrated with Madeline's apathy, but he was far too godly of a man to lash out at her. "Doctor Parker speaks out of frustration," he answered calmly without tossing Madeline under the bus. "I believe she is concerned that you will not believe us regardless of the truth we speak and assumes that we will be killed."

"Actually, I could care less if they decide to kill me," Madeline argued with a sigh. "I'm more worried they will kill you or John."

Antonio drew in a breath to steady his own patience. "The Blood," he said with a sigh, attempting to return to the topic at hand. "It is not blood as you know it, but I regret it is more difficult to explain than the misunderstanding of language. I am more than happy to explain, but it is not a quick reply and requires study." "Give them the Protestant version," Madeline chimed, causing Antonio to recoil in personal displeasure. Madeline smirked again. "It is just wine," she continued, looking at Robin. "It symbolizes the blood of god spilled to redeem his followers of their sins. It symbolizes Salvation. You know, the reason we're all here?" The accusatory tone was not lost on anyone.

"Oh," Robin said, thinking he understood. "Yours is a warrior god! Then you remember his sacrifice in battle by consuming the symbolic wine? This is more understandable. Heironeious has a similar demand."

Antonio looked sour as Madeline handed him a pleased expression. "It... there is a considerable theological discourse behind what Doctor Parker has said," came his quiet reply. It wasn't the correct explanation, but it was offered quickly enough to satisfy the crisis.

"What is a Protestant?" Simon asked, obviously not missing the silent disagreement between the two in question.

"It is another sect of the broader religion, Christianity. We follow the teachings of Christ, ergo, the blood of Christ," Antonio answered easily. "There are theological disagreements between our two sects," he added to explain the disconnect.

"If the wine is symbolic, then you would have no problem with it being disposed of," Tracy stated, thinking she had caught them in some trick.

Antonio offered her a patient, though saddened smile as Madeline flashed her one of fury. "I would insist it be disposed of in a manner consistent with our faith if this is required," he answered gently. "If this would aid in arriving at an understanding, I will do so, and any are welcome to witness the event." Madeline's angry look shifted to Antonio before again retreating to apathy. Several people seemed to relax as the priest volunteered to dispose of the blood.

"You have asked the wrong questions," came the sing-song voice of a woman with a shaved head and dressed in white robes. "This man speaks the truth. The truth is from what he knows to be true, just as all here speak the truth as they know it to be true. The question to be asked is why these many truths appear false to those who hear them?"

Robin lifted both eyebrows as he turned to regard the wise woman. "This is great wisdom," he offered in regard. "May I ask your name, miss?"

"I am Sister Lili Wen, head monk of the Order of Light atop Mount Cerilos in Sarlona. Our order professes peace and practices the way of the Unseen Eye." Lili was not surprised that no one had heard of her, though Istvan's face was immediately lit with understanding. He knew where Sarlona was and had even heard of the Order of Light.

"Have we sufficiently addressed your concerns?" Madeline asked pointedly of Simon. "Can we go?" The tone was exactly what Istvan worried would happen, and Robin's expression mirrored {Istvan's disappointment.

Natalia answered on Simon's behalf. "The wrong is on our hands," she said sadly.

"No shit," Madeline replied tersely as she rose to walk to the closet, which was being thoroughly guarded by Thorn, the Dwarven-speaking man, and another assaulted on the other end by John. "Step aside," she told them in a tone that brokered no discussion.

"No," Simon replied from behind her. He would never have admitted it, but Madeline had earned herself a great deal of respect from the man. She handled herself like his equal and commanded the power she naturally wielded effortlessly. The men made an uncomfortable appearance, not knowing what to do.

It was a man with the most striking blue eyes Madeline had ever seen who decided to speak. "As she says," he said, gesturing to Natalia, "The wrong is on our hands. So are the consequences."

"If you release him now, there will be violence. It can be avoided by permitting him time to gather his senses." While Simon respected Madeline, he had none for John.

"So, you would remove his freedoms because the consequences of this farse are uncomfortable to you?" Inquired a woman who had been quiet until then. The statement was completely insulting to Simon and Tracy as well. "This sounds like a problem that an Archduke ought to be able to handle," she continued fluidly.

Madeline cocked an eyebrow at the woman. She couldn't help but agree with her, offering her an appraising look. Antonio sighed heavily. "This land is intended to be perfect," he said in frustration while crossing the room to John's prison. "It has already seen far too much senseless violence. John," he called into the screaming mess on the other side of the door. "John, please calm down," he begged. "Madeline and I have been unharmed. They have agreed to release you if you can agree to restrain your violence-"

"I'll fook'n kill e'ry last one of 'em!" John managed to articulate.

"Fey man in a rage," the barbarian named Thorn commented. There were a few shrugs as if this seemed to make perfect sense. Thorn frowned. He wondered what it would be like to be in a rage and be contained like John. Thorn suspected that it would only make it worse.

Madeline also frowned. "No, you aren't," Madeline snapped at John harshly. "You're gonna calm your ass down this second, and we're gonna walk out of here, got it?"

The assault on the door stopped, but John was still breathing heavily from the other side. "Good," Madeline told him. "Now we're going to open this door, and you'll listen to whatever Father Antonio tells you to do, understand?"

'What are they gonna do to us?" He demanded.

"Nothing. Father Antonio took care of it. Talked them down. They all agree that they are idiots and are very sorry about this. Now, the good father has gone through a lot of trouble to get us out of here without having to throw a punch, and frankly, John, looking at these guys out here..." She eyed the three men, skeptical that John would be able to take all three of them at once. If Maddy had to guess, their biceps were bigger than her thigh.

"Fook that shit, Maddy," John hissed in reply. "I'm the Irish fook'n-"

"Bomber, yes, I know," Madeline interrupted, sounding bored. "Can we just try this the priest's way, please?" It wasn't so much a plead as a patronizing demand which elicited a smirk on the corner of Simon's lips. "He's good at compromises, in case you didn't notice. Anyway, his way involves all three of us walking out of here and puts you in a much better position for protecting us than trying to take on three NFL linebackers at once. Seriously, will you assholes step away?" She asked forcefully of the three men at the door. The blue-eyed man cocked an eyebrow, but Thorn looked impressed. "It's not like he will come barreling out knowing that Antonio and I are standing right here. Isn't that right, John?"

"Why the fook would I hurt ya when I'm try'n ta get out ta save ya!" He snapped back in irritation.

"Precisely my point," she agreed while casting an incredulous look to those defying her. "Move. Now."

"Let fey man out," Thorn said firmly. "He no evil, no be in a little cage. This bad. Kord no wants." Thorn moved out of the way, intent on opening the door himself, when he was interrupted.

Antonio didn't wait for an answer and stepped forward and pulled open the door, instantly positioning himself between John and the others. As expected, John lunged forward, his bright face red from the fury he was experiencing, and his hands dripped with blood from his escape attempt. While not a violent man, Antonio grabbed him to attempt to hold him back from the others. "You fook'n bastards!" John hissed in one of the only intelligible things to come out of his mouth.

CHAPTER 2

"We're leaving," Madeline announced as she turned and glared so strongly that a path naturally cleared for her. Antonio kept his hold on John and directed him through the path and out the door, the Three disappearing into the white afternoon light.

There was a silence left in their wake. "Well." commented the beautiful woman as she offered a sultry but sarcastic smile. "You boys made quite a mess of that one. If it is to his Highness's approval, I will be following suit," she concluded, offering a charming smirk to Simon.

"I have no regrets if that is what you imply, miss," Simon answered under an arched brow. "I will do all that is necessary to protect this world from Evil as that is what the Saint demanded of us, lest any choose to forget it. To question me is to question he who positioned me here." The undertone of Cuthbertian fascism was undeniable. There was certainly a battle looming on the horizon.

"Wait for me," called the woman Madeline had offered high regard. She quickly followed the beautiful woman, and the two disappeared without further comment.

"Salvation, they said. A new start." Istvan let out an ire after the Three had departed.

Straightening up, he made his way to where Robin stood, looking utterly out of control.

"We have been here less than an hour, and already we have managed to alienate three who would seek the same. Others as well, if their departures are to be taken in kind. In case no one has looked or listened, if we take what the Gods have told us as fact, at least until it is disproven, they brought us here to start anew. This sort of behavior cannot be tolerated if we are to form a community. We must be cooperative to make this a place where our future children can thrive," he explained, not one comfortable speaking at length, as his voice rose and fell, steady in places and shaky in others. He tended to ramble, but he did not like where the common feeling was headed, so he stepped up.

"We all come from different lands, most likely, as not all of our Patrons are commonly known to one another. It makes sense that different languages would be spoken in those lands, evolved from different needs. Who is to say that one who speaks in the tongue of Dragons is less worthy than one who speaks the tongues of Elves or Dwarves...or Men, for example? I urge you to put aside the petty attitudes that plagued our world and approach this new one with an open mind.", he finished, seeming abashed to have been so public and squinting his eyes slightly as he awaited the inevitable reproaches.

"And you would have us cast aside reason?" Countered Tracy firmly. "Speaking in the ilkish tongue of a Dragon is one matter, Mr. Caracus, but speaking in the tongues of devils is an entirely different issue. No," she said with some finality, "the nobility will decide which course of action ought to be taken."

This statement instantly polarized the group for several reasons. In reality, very few had ever given a question to whether or not the nobles would rule, but it was not something that Istvan could swallow easily. His green eyes met hers in a hard gaze of determination. "Forgive me, m'Lady, but I was unaware that there was anything other than an empty village awaiting us here. Perhaps I was not present; which lord of this land knighted you thusly?"

Tracy's eyes were reduced to slits as she took in Istvan without intimidation. "Your talk of abandoning titles and structure would lead us directly into chaos and darkness. Such cannot be tolerated in any world if it is to remain pure."

"Why?" came a rather blunt question from Thorn.

"What do you mean, why?" Asked Jacelyn innocently. "Any thriving community must have order."

"You say. But this is not good—this law. Not same," the brute replied.

"This fellow is correct," said a cleric who had until now been silent. "The natural world has no order and only the most basic rules. Your statements would imply that the wilderness is inherently evil. I am Ananda, a servant of the Obad-hai. This man is Thorn, a devotee of Kord and wiser than you credit him."

Simon rolled his eyes. "I believe I have heard enough." He turned, gesturing for a few others to follow, and he, Jacelyn, and Tracy left the temple.

"W-wait!" Called Robin after them, but the man with the striking blue eyes rested his hand on the young man's arm. This man had a stature similar to the dwarven-speaking man and had been one of the men keeping John in his little cage.

"It is noble that you put forth the effort, my young friend, but some things cannot be changed. Followers of St. Cuthbert are one of them. My name is Timius of Sexton. I am a cleric of Erathus. You needn't worry," he added with a glance to Ananda, "for not all here care for such strong impositions of law."

"I agree with Timius, young Robin," replied Lili sadly. "There are those who seek to impose order, those who would replace it with chaos, and those of us caught in between."

Those who remained continued to talk as Robin had hoped, discussing their situation. In the end, they agreed that all of the clerics would remain in the temple to pray to the gods in hopes of further clarity and that the scholars would look for answers in arcane magics and mundane knowledge. The others would establish the town to ensure that all had enough to eat and were properly clothed and housed.

It was only as the group was finally starting to disperse (having lost almost half of the others) that Albus gently stopped Istvan. "My friend, it was unwise of you to announce your positions before those such as the Cuthberts," he said cautiously. "Even if the words you spoke were wise indeed. I do not believe that speaking a language does one evil. It is how one behaves which determines this, and it is quite possible that the stranger folk among us are from a strange and far-off land where such oddities are commonplace. It is not our duty to judge these people harshly, but rather, affirm the goodness within them. It appears we are kindred spirits. I shall look forward to working with you."

Istvan deflated slightly. "I suppose you are correct, and it does please me to call you a friend as well," he admitted. Istvan let out a heavy sigh. "What are we to do? I suppose the arcane explorations are left to us?"

Albus smiled at him. "I shall return to the library and begin a study of my own," he replied mildly conspiratorially. "I believe a strong scry would be of use here," he added with a wink. Albus was content with hiding that he was a wizard for as long as possible, though Istvan was already well aware.

Istvan offered him a grin as he followed him back to the library. He already decided that he liked the man, and, somehow, Istvan thought him a fatherly sort. An idea suddenly came to the man, and he snapped his fingers. "The genders are even," he commented, still processing the thought. "Are we meant to form pairs? It would seem yes if we are to repopulate this land..." Istvan suddenly found himself wondering which of the women would be his mate.

In his mind, he had already eliminated Tracy and Jacelyn. While Jacelyn at least was lovely, neither women's disposition had appealed to him. Natalia and Lili were attractive and seemingly wise, as were the others. Still, Istvan's mind drifted to two specific women: Madeline and the beautiful woman who had not offered her name.

Istvan was so deep in thought that he did not notice when Madeline quietly stepped into the library. Albus stopped what he was working on to look up at her. She frowned upon seeing Albus and Istvan. "Did you finish checking the books?" She demanded more than asked.

Albus shook his head. "I am afraid they are all blank, m'Lady." He watched her curiously.

"Can I have one?" She asked, which seemed to surprise Albus.

"M'Lady, they are not mine but the property of all here," he answered.

Istvan's eyes instantly locked on Madeline in the sense of hope that the notion of the community hadn't been lost in this terrible misunderstanding. "Miss... er... Doctor? Parker?" He stumbled over his words, suddenly feeling rather lame.

Madeline offered him a skeptical look but waited for him to finish.

"I... about before... we didn't..." He stammered. This was quite unlike him. Istvan was usually quite logical and diplomatic.

The skeptical look didn't diminish. She gave him a look long enough to silently communicate that she thought him a fool before she returned to address Albus. "I didn't know if anyone had established any claims to property, and the last thing I need right now is to be accused of stealing," she told him frankly. "So, can I have a blank book and maybe a pen or something too?"

Albus looked slightly deflated, but he offered her a compliant smile as he rose to fetch a spare ink well and a fresh quill. Madeline looked at the quill and, well, incredulously. "I... wow...uh " It was her turn to fumble over her words, though she did appear to be attempting to be polite.

Albus offered her another smile, though this one was laced with confusion. "Is the ink not to your liking, m'Lady? I am afraid it is the only ink I have found in the library."

Madeline gave him a mildly pathetic look. "I honestly have no idea," she replied genuinely. "I've never used a feather before...

Istvan offered Albus a confused look. "Forgive me, Doctor Parker," he started, assuming Doctor was her title, "But are you not a noble? You have the demeanor of an educated woman, and your priest attributes you a title ?"

Madeline raised both eyebrows in surprise. "A what?" She repeated, obviously further confused. "Uh... no. I'm..." Madeline abandoned the effort at that point, retreating into her comfortable level of apathy. "Nevermind. No, I'm not a noble, yes, I'm educated, and that doesn't mean I instantly know how to use this. It doesn't matter. I'm sure this will do; thanks," she said, awkwardly accepting the ink and quill and tucking a book under her arm.

Madeline moved toward the door when Istvan stood to approach her. Again, she gave him a skeptical look. "Wait, Madeline," he insisted, rounding a table to stand next to her. "Did you find a cabin for yourself and your friends? Umm, the father? Maybe I could walk you home? It is getting dark out. I promise to be a gentleman.", he spouted out much less elegantly than he had wanted. He did not want to scare or offend her, hoping to recover from the massive faux pax that the group had committed earlier.

Madeline offered him a plane look. "The cabins are marked," she replied, much to Istvan's and Albus's surprise. "I found what seems to be mine, thank you." She had the terse politeness of a general as if the business of social interaction was a laborious endeavor to her, and she took great pains to avoid it if she could. "Anyway, I'm not afraid of the dark," she added. Something suggested a dual meaning to the statement. "Thanks for the offer, but it's unnecessary." She nodded over to one of the other stores. "Maybe one of the women would like that, though. That Jacelyn chick probably would," she added, curiously removing herself from that designation and distancing herself from the other obvious noble.

The fact that they were having a conversation, even as awkward as it was, felt like a victory to the man. They had lost so much in what Simon had conducted in the temple, and Istvan suspected it would take months, maybe years, to unravel. As Madeline turned to leave again, Istvan started after her again, instantly regretting it. He was beginning to look needy.

"Oh, alright. That is a far walk, but if you are comfortable with it... You know, I am something of a scholar myself... I would be happy to lend my expertise if you intend to author something. I think Albus is working on a book of known spells to be shared and a bestiary of known animals and monstrous creatures from the.... home. It might be fun to exchange knowledge", he called out more gently, pausing to gather his thoughts before finishing.

Madeline's expression went blank as if she was trying to decide whether Istvan was a fool or he was genuine. That was not an expression he was accustomed to receiving. Usually, he was on the other end of it. "A spell book, huh?" She asked, implying right away what she thought was ridiculous. "I uh... I'm going to have to pass, Mr. Caracus," she replied as politely as she could. "Thanks anyway.... uhm... have a nice evening?" She seemed unsure of herself, but not in a weak sense. In form, Madeline was a delicate and beautiful woman. In personality, she could rival Simon and probably any general Istvan had ever met. The two did not seem to fit together at all.

With that said, Madeline turned and left, this time for good, leaving Istvan feeling childish and embarrassed for his efforts. Albus stepped into the doorway of the library as the woman walked away. He watched her with interest, though the look was more scrutinizing and suspicious than appraising. He only broke his study to eye Istvan.

"I would not take an interest in her, my good friend," he advised solemnly and quietly. "My scries are not yet complete, but what has transpired thus far suggests she is far more than any have expected."

Istvan looked concerned as his friend closed the door. "She isn't evil after all, is she?" He was almost afraid to know.

"No, no," Albus said with a gentle smile and a dismissive gesture. "The results of my scry, however, were more than I expected. Of course, I could not in good conscience limit my efforts to the Three. I am scrying everyone; I trust this does not offend you..." Albus paused long enough to take in Istvan's reply.

Istvan smiled and sat at one of the seats. "Of course not. I believe it will go a long way toward building trust once you share your results," he added.

"That, perhaps, is not wise for the moment," Albus cautioned. The old man let out a tired sigh as he sat opposite Istvan. "The paladin, Tracy, is what I feared," he revealed. "In my world, the Cuthbertians made it a crime to cast arcanely. They imprisoned or killed any mage who was unwilling to collar themselves."

"Wait, what?" Istvan returned, suddenly finding himself very confused. "On your world? Collar? I fear you are speaking too quickly for me, Dellebian," he answered, adding what he assumed would be a compliment.

It worked, and Albus smiled more patiently. "The largest result of my scry is that we are all from different worlds. It would explain the differences, the unfamiliarities in deities, and the like. I suppose a discerning mind would arrive at this without magic, but we do not have such a luxury here. Lady Tracy and I are from the same world. It is similar to many others, but the Cuthbertians have an iron rule on many of the lands there. They despise Arcane magic because they cannot control it. A Collar was crafted, nullifying magical fields and preventing the wearer from channelling mana. Only a wizard of the first order could have removed the collar," he added with a glimmer in his eyes. Apparently, the collar had posed little challenge to the old man

"It would be dangerous for me to reveal my particular set of skills, my friend, and you as well. With Simon as her aid, those two will seek to establish their strict laws here, fueled by their fear of chaos. We will be more aid in resisting that if we are not immediate targets," he added.

Istvan was still reeling about the different worlds. It made sense, but he had only ever heard of spell jamming in passing; he had never thought to experience it. "Did... then we did die?" He inquired, unsure of himself.

Albus nodded. "It would appear we all passed. From what I have uncovered, the demons conducted an orchestrated attack on as many worlds as possible. We all fought in the same war on many different worlds, and in some cases, planes. I did not cry long enough to gather details on these worlds themselves, only that they exist. My focus was more on those who are here now and who they were on their own worlds so that we can put this business of evil to rest once and for all."

"Well?" Istvan inquired, now intrigued, "Who were we?"

Albus leaned back in his chair. "Everyone was important. Many here have managed to kill a demon. Thorn, for example, strangled one to death." Istvan was just as impressed as Albus. This was not a trivial feat; only a great warrior could kill a demon alone.

"There were only three here who managed to kill more than one of the demons, and two of them are among the Three," he revealed, causing a chill to run down Istvan's spine. Killing one Demon unassisted was the stuff of epic legends. Was he killed more than one? That wasn't possible for a human.

"The priest of the Three, Antonio, was a leader in their religion. He was apparently well known and sacrificed himself to the demons, hoping to spare lives. It was.....inspirationally selfless. The man is a pacifist, and as a follower of Rao, I believe you will appreciate his love of community," Albus stopped to take a drink from his mug. It smelled like a cider of some sort.

"The young man, John, was some criminal before the war. This is where I become confused, I am afraid. They are from the Mechanus plane. The machines they have, Istvan... it is simply daunting. John used a machine to create an explosion which killed 15 demons at once. I will attempt to draw what I have seen. As an Artificer, perhaps you will have more insight into its function..."

Istvan's eyes went wide, and he lost all awareness of anything except Albus. "Did... did I hear you correctly? That hot-headed fey man killed fifteen demons?" Istvan was at a loss for words.

Albus nodded solemnly. "He was easier to scry than the others because Doctor Parker called him the Irish Bomber. I am afraid I cannot tell you how many she killed, but it was more than John. The same is true for the cleric of Erathus, Timius. He and Madeline killed the most of any here, but I do not know how they accomplished this."

Istvan leaned back in his chair, words simply not coming to him. "And we accused her of being evil.... we are such fools..."

Albus nodded in agreement. "John was nothing more than a common thug, but Madeline was apparently their world leader," he revealed. "Doctor is her title. Given the nature of her accomplishments with the demons, I suggest we use it." The statement had dual meaning, but Istvan didn't have to reflect to understand that Albus was on the fence about whether or not they should respect titles. "At this stage, I have determined everyone's name, homeworld, and a simple fact about them. I will learn more in time."

Albus took a piece of parchment from the desk where apparently, he had spelt a quill to write for him while he dealt with other issues. On it was a list of names, as Albus had promised:

Madeline Ann Parker, Yawey, Earth, Balanced Goodness

John Simon Reece, Yawey, Earth, Chaotic Goodness

Antonio Manuel Phillipe Maria Del Fonte, Cleric of Yawey, Earth, Orderly Goodness

Istvan of Caracus, Rao, Eberron, Balanced Goodness

Lili Wen, Iluminus, Eberron, Balanced Goodness

Robin Tenderfoot, Cleric of Heironeous, Oerth, Orderly Goodness

Ananda Rhanf, Cleric of Obad Hai, Oerth, Chaotic Goodness

Tracy Quickfeather, Saint Cuthbert, Abeir-Toril, Orderly Goodness

Albus Zediphorus, Delleb, Abeir-Toril, Balanced Goodness

Jacelyn of Brandonia, Rao, Tellene, Orderly Goodness

Landia Q'nyer of Rean, Obad Hai, Tellene, Chaotic Goodness

Bella La Folia, Gadhelyn, Krynn, Chaotic Goodness

Timius of Sexton, Cleric of Erathus, Krynn, Balanced Goodness

Natalia Romanofski, Cleric of Sarenrae, Glorion, Balanced Goodness

Sylvia of the Wood, Elhonna, Glorion, Chaotic Goodness

Thorn, Kord, Mystara, Chaotic Goodness

Thadeus Smyth, Moradin, Mystara, Balanced Goodness

Simon of Trent, Saint Cuthbert, Onara, Orderly Goodness

Istvan frowned and ran his hand across his mouth. "This scry has uncovered more questions than answers." So many worlds were present, and he knew of none of them. There were many clerics and likely a few paladins from what he already knew. That made sense, given the nature of the war.

"True, but such is the case with Delleb," Albus replied. "Fortunately, I learned that all here are of good inclinations. All that varies is our disposition toward order, though, as you can see, you and I are similarly inclined, and those of balanced thought outnumber the others. I also know that the monkish woman called Lili is of your world. She was the most difficult to scry as her deity was more a philosophy than an entity; as such, it is a new god in this place. Perhaps you knew her?"

Istvan shook his head. "I did not. I would wish to speak with her, though. That another is here from Eberron gives me a measure of comfort. Perhaps I shall speak with her" Istvan studied the list, frowning as he realized Albus's world-mate. "Not Tracy..."

Albus looked a bit disappointed. "Unfortunately, it is true, though I appear to be the only loyalist of Delleb. I was interested to see your match is Queen Jacelyn," he added with a smirk.

Istvan rolled his eyes. One of the nobles advocated class rule. Of course.

"Timius, the cleric who killed many demons and Bella, the beautiful woman from the temple, are also from the same world. Krynn, I believe it was called. It is a land filled with Dragons; I would not be surprised if either were a half-dragon or even full, given that particular land." There was a continent of Dragons on Eberron, so this did not cause Istvan a reason for concern, but he assumed that the Cuthbertians would not be pleased if they ever learned there was a dragon among them.

Mentioning the woman caused Istvan's heart to stir, though he hardly knew why. Of all the women here, Bella was the most beautiful. Madeline and Jacelyn were closely tied for second, but Bella's lead was obvious. Everything about her was utterly stunning, and Istvan suddenly found himself daydreaming about her.

There was a sound of heavy boots as Timius pushed open the Library door. The enormous cleric practically dominated the space as he entered. "Albus. Istvan," he offered with a nod to each of them. "I was wondering if I may see a copy of the religious text of the three," he said, going straight to the point.

Albus frowned slightly and shook his head. "The young noblewoman took them with her," Albus answered. "She was concerned after the Paladin Tracy demanded they be burnt, and Dr Parker wished to protect them."

Timius frowned and seemed to consider the men for a moment. "That is unacceptable. As mages, I do not doubt that you would be able to decipher the text magically," he said again, making no attempt to guise his intentions. "We have been unable to discern alignment. I believe this would be one avenue toward making this determination. The texts are required." He glanced around the room for a moment, noticing where Albus had set up his writing desk.

In the meantime, Albus kept a straight face, though he was less pleased to have the cleric put him in such a way. "You do understand what such a description of a scholar may imply to certain.... parties... I presume?"

"Of course," Timius answered. "Fortunately, few gods support the methods of the Cuthbertians, mage, just as there are few Cuthbertians able to see through the cunning of an intelligent Dellebian seeking anonymity. You are no doubt studying as a means to uncover the purpose of our placement here. What have you learned?"

Timius was probably the tersest person Istvan had ever encountered.

Albus seemed to consider the question for a moment. "I have not yet concluded the scrying," he answered. "But I have learned that all here are who they claim to be."

Timius nodded, and Albus slid the parchment across the table. Timius frowned. "This script is unfamiliar to me," he revealed. "What language is it penned?"

Albus raised both eyebrows. "In the common --" Albus interrupted himself with a pause. "I am afraid I have channelled too much mana this day as it is. Tomorrow I could provide you with a spell to re-"

"That is unnecessary," Timius interrupted flatly. "Have you learned the inclinations and deities of those represented here?"

Albus nodded. "Yes, and more," he answered, reading the list to Timius, who frowned in confusion.

"We do not hail from the same world," he stated in the same flat tone. "Who knows of this?"

"Only us, as far as I know," Istvan said curiously. "But I believe our Dellebian friend will insist that everyone be informed," he added as Albus nodded in agreement.

Timius was a man who seemed to value justice but who also was not likely to tolerate any level of foolishness. He was straightforward and did not mask any aspect of what he said. He frowned. "The clerics have discussed a means of remedying the wrongs which were conducted toward the Three earlier. We believe that if smaller parties were to approach them in a friendly manner, they would be more receptive to us, and the damage can be undone slowly. The previous misunderstanding was severe and stemmed from confusion. Complicating the matter by introducing another source of confusion, that we are from multiple worlds, is unwise for the moment. It would be best to allow tempers to settle before this announcement."

Istvan frowned but said nothing. He couldn't see a fault in Timius's statement, and the man wasn't advocating keeping it a secret forever. Rather, he was trying to preserve the community, which was certainly an end Istvan wanted to see.

"In the meantime, it would be a boon if those texts could be recovered," Timius stated, turning to leave.

"What shall become of them after they have been translated?" Albus asked seriously.

Timius looked at him squarely. "It depends on the nature of the text. If it declares them evil, it will be destroyed with them. If it vindicates them, then it shall be returned to them. Discretion would be of value in this matter." Timius didn't elaborate and simply turned to leave.

Istvan sighed heavily as the imposing man left. "My friend, this is as much as I can withstand for one day. I believe I will retire to what is to be my cabin. I shall assist you with this inquiry in the morn."

At that, Istvan rose, dismissing himself, and wandering off into the budding darkness. There was a light in the distance, across a lake, which drew him unconsciously to it. It was a walk which took him nearly twenty minutes. The air was cool and refreshing, but it did nothing to ease his mind. The light grew larger as he approached, revealing first that it was a part of a structure and then that it was a window, leaking the light into the deep darkness surrounding the structure.

As he approached, Istvan knew right away that he should look aside. From within the building, Madeline was discarding her last piece of clothing and tying her long brown hair up, preparing to step into a bath. Istvan was a gentleman and knew better than to watch a lady as he was, but all the same, his eyes were hopelessly locked on the nude form, preparing to bathe.

Istvan's eyes were wide, and unable to look away. The war on Eberron had taken so much... Their freedoms, sure, but simple things as well. Istvan realized, watching Madeline, that he could not remember the last time he had been with a woman, and as he became aware of this, he also realized how quickly his body was responding to the visage before him.

Madeline's form was slender and sleek; her movements fluid as she bent to test the water of the tub she had drawn for her bath. Carefully, her hands swept Chestnut locks upward, tying them delicately atop her head.

The movement caused her tits to bounce slightly against her chest. It was here that Istvan's eyes lingered. Perfectly sized ivory orbs, marked in the centre by a coin-sized circle. Her nipples had already hardened from the cool springtime air around her, and Istvan's hands ached to run over them.

Her chest tapered into a curved waist and then expanded over smooth hips. At her joining was a mound of dark hair, forming a perfect triangle against her alabaster thighs.

The woman was utterly unaware that she was being watched, and she carefully tested the water with her hand while sitting alongside the tub. Finding it to her liking, Madeline brought her feet over the edge one at a time and then slid into the steaming water with a relaxed sigh.

There were thick woods behind the cabin; before he knew it, Istvan had slipped behind it and was peering into a window he had no business looking into. Only the sudden words from behind gave him what he needed to stop staring.

"Like what you see, do you?" Asked the voice of Bella from behind him. She smirked and cocked an eyebrow at him. "We could share, I suppose," she suggested with a nod toward the window. "But then, I'm not always the sharing type."

The woman smiled at him as she turned to walk deeper into the woods, suggesting he would be the world's biggest idiot if he didn't follow after her leaving Istvan torn between humiliation and intrigue.

Ultimately, curiosity won out. Istvan blushed and looked from the window to the woman and then back and again before he rushed after her, scratching his scalp nervously.

"Share? I mean, you will not tell her what I saw you? Keep it between us." he asked and insisted, unsure why they were headed into the woods, but his eyes then paid attention to her form, and he needed no further urging. The last stages of the demonic invasion robbed everyone of the time or desired to enjoy more pleasurable pursuits.

Bella stopped and smiled confidently. "I suppose that depends on what you are willing to do to ensure my mouth is kept shut," she suggested, stopping in a small clearing and turning to face him as she slowly untied the top of her dress in a rather enticing manner.

"My silence could be bought for an hour or so of... service," she replied in a saucy tone. "Presuming I find the required service satisfactory, you have paid for my silence regarding your indiscretion with the lady's privacy." She wagged her finger at him as if to mock him for misbehaving. In the process, the dress slid neatly off of her form, with no shyness whatsoever on her part.

If Madeline's naked form had aroused him, Istvan would have been helpless in the presence of a goddess like Bella. Rather than sleek, Bella was curved in all the right places. Her large breasts fell against her chest with a bounce, and a gentle breeze pushed her scent of arousal to Istvan's awaiting nose. He stood, for a moment, gazing in awe at Bella's stunning beauty before swallowing hard.

Bella cocked a brow at him. "Your trousers are still affixed, Mr Carcosa," she replied seductively.

I... yes," he answered, instantly fumbling with the belt.

Bella offered him a chuckle and strode forward, casually swaying her hips. She easily fell to her knees and carefully pulled Istvan's enlarged dick free. She smiled as if pleasantly surprised. "It appears our noblewoman has aroused you well," she murmured as she ran her tongue up the length of his shaft.

Istvan released a sharp gasp at the sensation, forcing himself to endure it long enough to bury himself inside this surprising woman. Bella offered a devilish grin at his reply and kept her light brown eyes directed upward as she drew his head into her mouth.

Bella let out a pleased moan, swishing her tongue back and forth across his thickness as she took as much of him into her mouth as she could. Anything that wouldn't fit was treated to her hands, gently massaging his swollen balls and stroking along his base.

Istvan's hands pushed forward by instinct alone, tangling in Bella's hair. It had been such a long time, and Bella's mouth was perfectly warm and wet, her tongue more talented than any woman he had ever bedded. Istvan was almost unaware that he let out a deep, satisfied groan of approval, and he certainly wasn't conscious of the gentle back-and-forth rhythm he was beginning to develop with her mouth.

With each pass of her tongue, Bella was driving Istvan mad. Within a matter of moments, his thrusting became more insistent, and soon, he was trying to pull out of her mouth. Much to his horror, Bella would not allow it. "I... I'm... I- Uhhhhh" He couldn't finish the thought before his first wave of hot seed splashed into her mouth and down her throat.

Bella swallowed and suckled until she had finished every last drop. Istvan collapsed to his knees in exhaustion.

"I don't think so," Bella teased, easing him to his back. Istvan hardened again almost instantly.

Bella straddled him and began nibbling on his neck as she slid his hardened length into her steamy folds. Bella's arousal was undeniable, and as her velvety lips wrapped around his thick cock, Istvan half wondered if he would come prematurely just at the bliss of the sensation.

She pulled herself up so that only the head remained inside before dropping down hard, impaling herself on his length. Both she and Istvan let out a cry with each feverish stroke.

As their rhythm began to crescendo again, Istvan bucked his hips to impale her harder and harder. The woman was in ecstasy about it.

"Come on," He urged, watching as her tits bounced each time he thrust hard into her waiting sex. "Come on. Give it to me."

"Harder. Harder!" She cried out. "Oh, Gadhelyn... Fuck me, Harder!" She almost screamed.

Istvan continued to thrust harder and harder into her until their bodies slapping echoed in the glade around him.

Suddenly, Bella's eyes burst open, and she gasped in desperation. Istvan was already on the verge of coming a second time when he felt her walls begin to clamp down around him. It was all he needed to throw him over the edge, and he sprayed into her depths as her womanhood clenched furiously to his dick.

Bella collapsed, panting in delight into his ear as Istvan found himself seeing stars. The woman was amazing, far beyond anyone he had ever experienced. At this moment, he knew she was who the gods had intended for his mate.

"I hope you are not finished," she panted with a smile. "You are far too delectable not to enjoy all night."

Istvan smiled at her, running his hand gently over her raven hair. "How shall I take you now, lover?" He inquired in a husky tone.

Bella leaned in, her breath tickling his ear. "In the manner, you imagined taking her," she offered. "We shall have her together," she volunteered. "I will make her do amazing things for you, my dear."

Istvan lost his smile at the implication, but he was already hardening again. "I... I uh..."

Bella merely smiled. "In time, in time. For now, it seems as though I must relieve you again."

Istvan frowned again, now wondering if the woman wasn't manipulating him for some end. Frustrated, he pushed her off him and then forced her to flip to her hands and knees. In an instant, he was behind her, positioning his thick head in her swollen and drenched pussy.

"And I may have you any manner I wish?" He inquired in a hot voice that spoke of power.

"Oh please," she let out, her lips quivering in anticipation around his head.

Istvan clamped his hands onto her hips. He'd figure out her intentions later. For now, he needed this release. He needed it hard and fast.

In a powerful trust, Istvan pushed all the way in and pulled nearly out. Bella gasped at being so utterly filled in one moment and then empty again in another. "I wonder... will you come when I wish it?" Istvan pondered as he continued pumping into her, each time taking her breath away.

Bella grinned despite herself. "Is that how you like it?" She asked, almost rhetorically. "But of course, master," she replied in a perfectly submissive voice.

Istvan quivered slightly. Bella was gifted at making love, and it could take him a lifetime to become her equal. Rather than becoming daunted at the mere thought of her potential, Istvan focused on the present. He continued to slam into her, feeling her become more and more aroused with each powerful thrust.

"Beg me!" He cried out, almost unable to contain his own lust any further. "Ask for it-"

"Oh Please!" she nearly screamed. "Please let me come! Let me come, and let me suck your dick again, please!"

Istvan was already reeling from the pleasure. He reached around to grope her large breasts and guided her hips to obey their thrusts. Finding her nipple already hard, he pinched it until she cried out, writhing against him in unbridled passion.

"So be it," he replied.

Bella let out another impassioned cry as her orgasm ripped through her. Istvan felt her vaginal walls clamp down around him, offering her grunts of approval as he continued his thrusting.

When her orgasm was complete, Bella pushed him back and instantly swallowed his entire length. Her head bobbed obediently along his shaft, urging him to fuck her face as he pleased.

Istvan did not disappoint. Her mouth was truly a treat, and he meant to experience it as often as possible. This time, he latched onto her face and took more control, truly fucking her mouth for maximum pleasure. "Oh, Bella," he let out. "Oh, you feel so amazing..."

Bella was exhausted but diligent. While Istvan manned the pumping, her hands again went to attend to his balls and the base of his shaft while her tongue swished to and fro. She added enough suction with her mouth, and Istvan let out a pleased moan.

Within seconds, he was coming again, shooting hot cum down Bella's throat and filling her mouth. The stimulation was nearly too much for the man, and the moment he had filled her again, his eyes rolled back, and Istvan passed out from fatigue...

The sun had begun peeking over the mounting when Istvan opened his eyes. Bella lay by his side, her sleeping chest's rhythmic rise and fall capturing his attention with a smile. The beauty blinked her eyes open, still tired from the evening escapades.

"Good morn," Istvan spoke softly as he brushed a stray lock from her face. It was obvious: he adored her.

"Mmmm, good morn indeed," she replied with a satisfied smile, though the tone was not what Istvan had expected. Rather than a gentle exchange of lovers, Bella's tone was friendly and dismissive, as if she were greeting him on the street and politely saying hello. "Hmmm. It is later than I expected," she commented, finding her dress and sliding it over her perfect form. "Much to do."

"W-wait... you are leaving?" Istvan called out as she stood to leave. The hurt in his voice was unmistakable.

"Of course," she answered as though she found the question to be an odd one. "Oh don't you worry, my dear. Your little indiscretion is quite safe with me. My lips are sealed."

"Have a nice day," she said in her standard silky tone as she sauntered into the woods. It didn't sort of saunter that demanded he follows after. Rather, it was the sort to imply his services were no longer required, and she was to be left in peace.

For the moment, Istvan just sat there. He was too stunned to move and felt utterly rejected. Had he not been a sufficient lover? There was no doubt that Bella was far more experienced than he, but she had come countless times; did that not mean she found him at least enjoyable?

After a few moments, he frowned and shook his head to dismiss these negative feelings. This was supposed to be paradise, but he was finding himself more miserable than not so far. After he had gathered and re-donned his garments, Istvan realized that he didn't fully know where he was. He knew that Maddy's cabin should be nearby, and as luck would have it, he began to overhear a conversation between her and John that led him from the woods. He paused as he neared, realizing that neither strange person knew he was present.

"What are you doin', lass?" John asked her, his accent the utter embodiment of the fey tongue. He was tugging a button-up shirt on over his bare chest, both it and his trousers looking far more normal by the standards of the rest of the villagers. On the other hand, Maddy was now clothed in something utterly foreign and more in line with what John had been wearing the previous day.

In place of her beautiful noble gown, Madeline now wore a short (by Istvan's standards) skirt, a tight-fitting blouse, and a heavy, blue canvas jacket. Skin-tight leggings partially covered her legs, and her shoes were the strangest contraptions Istvan had ever seen. She wore the garments comfortably and easily, indicating their familiarity with her.

"I'm weeding the garden," she answered John in a mildly cross tone.

"What on earth for?" He asked, flabbergasted. "Yer supposed to be find'n out whatever information ya can, not pull'n grass from a cabbage patch, for Christ's sake."

"All of the books were empty," she informed cooly, though calmly.

"And? And there ain't nooth'n else ya can be work'n on?" He returned, his voice starting to rise.

"Yeah. Weeding. What do you want me to do? They decided not to kill us. Great. You don't think that means they'll be all gung-ho about trading with us, do you?" She asked the question as if she thought John was an idiot. "Hell, that assumes they aren't some barter system, but I have no idea how economics would even work in a place like this. Did you see any money anywhere?"

John looked taken aback for a moment. "No, actually, I didn't," he remarked curiously.

"Yeah, me neither," she answered, returning to her garden. "So either there's some bank or something in town, which we obviously have no access to, ergo no money, or we just woke up in Barter-Ville, where everyone hates us and will probably not trade with us. Given that we only have about six months' worth of food between the three of us, no trading means no food. So, if we're going to eat, then, yeah. I'm weeding the fucking garden. Unless, of course, you'd like your second death to be starvation."

CHAPTER 3

John reached down and grabbed Maddy's arm, yanking her to her feet as she let out a surprised yelp. "Listen, lass," he said in a patient enough sounding voice. "We ain't gonna starve to death, do you understand me? They'll either come to their senses, or I'll make them. It don' matter which to me, but I do know a doctor has no business play'n house. You got better things to put that mind to, so it's more important that you go down to that library and play nice with the old fart and that weird fella to get all the information ya can, you understand? We gotta get outa here and you on your knees in the garden, pull'n out bits of grass sure as hell ain't gonna make that happen any faster."

Madeline's lips tightened as she tugged at his grip. Istvan couldn't quite make out her expression from his vantage point, but if it was anything like the one she had offered him for a similar gesture the night before, John should have been recoiled in intimidation right about now. Interestingly, he wasn't.

"Do you have any idea what you are saying?" She finally replied in a gravely serious voice. "I mean, you did see God yesterday, right?"

"What the fook does that gotta do with anything?" He barked in return, shaking her arm slightly to get a tighter grip.

Madeline's face contorted in disgusted disbelief. "Only God himself said we died and that he put us here intentionally, you moron," she countered in a brazen and fearless reply. Istvan winced on her behalf. It didn't take a genius to see where this was headed, and he suddenly felt Madeline was a fool for not backing down from John. "Even assuming I could build you some spaceship, which I can't, what makes you think escape is even possible, given that it was God who put us here in the first place?"

John's scowl was painful to watch, and Istvan winced for a second time, thinking he should probably intervene at some point. John pulled Madeline in closer, clearly exasperating the woman's obvious need for a sizable distance between her and anyone else. Madeline's face blushed red with anger as she doubled her efforts to escape fruitlessly. "Oh yeah?" He answered, his voice teetering on a dangerous calm before the storm. "I also watched them freak try ta kill us for reading the bible," he countered. "Ya think Gad intended on that? And all that talk about multiple gads... it's fook'n herasy, Madeline, and it doesn't take a genius like you to see that this ain't the paradise we were promised, which means it's all some alien fook'n trick. I'll bet we ain't even dead. I'll bet we're in some prison with our brains hooked up to some machine, pump'n all these thoughts inta our heads like some fook'n extended LSD trip from hell."

"If that's true, then nothing I do can wake us up," Madeline replied, the former bite to her tone now gone as if she had recognized the error in her approach too late.

John shrugged, offering her a little more space but not releasing her arm. "An' what if they dropped us on some alien planet or something? You pointed out the stars ain't where they ought to be," he added, much to Istvan's surprise. Albus had mentioned that it would take an observant and keen mind to discern that they were on another planet. If John's reply were to be taken seriously, Madeline had done so within a few hours of arriving here. "Maybe it's some Alien trick ta give us hope. Ya can't have misery without hope, and those fookers love misery," he concluded in what Istvan took as likely the most insightful thing the hothead had ever considered.

John tossed Maddy's arm back, causing her to stumble away slightly with far less grace than she had thus far demonstrated. "I don' much care about the why's," he said with finality. "All I care about is getting outa here and back home so we can give those alien fookers a taste of what the Irish Bomber can do when he ain't all beaten and bruised. The only one here who can do that is you and if you insist on need'n help, well, then train those two fookers at the library ta help ya. I'll warn ya, lass. I ain't gonna tolerate this foolery outa ya fer much longer, ya understand?"

Madeline scowled at him in return.

"I asked if ya understand, lass," He repeated in a serious tone.

"Yeah, I understand," she finally answered, none-too-happy about where this all had the lead.

"Good. Now get yer ass down there and get ta work. No more shitt'n around in the garden."

Madeline continued to give him a scowl as she non-committally stepped away and toward what Istvan assumed must have been the road. For his part, John moved in the opposite direction.

Istvan frowned as he took in the interaction as a whole. He did not care for the way John treated his companion. He had seen the type before, and sooner or later, it would escalate to physical violence. In any case, he would not interfere, not unless asked. They were both so strange to him that he didn't want to risk furthering the misunderstanding between the Three and the rest of them.

Giving the hothead time to distract himself, Istvan took a circular route back to the village, intersecting Madeline's path halfway there. Along the way, his mood soured considerably, largely owing to how John had treated Madeline and the impotence Istvan felt. The physical delight with Bella only lasted so long. It barely endured past her matter-of-fact dismissal of him.

Madeline had grabbed one of the books she had the night before and had tucked it under her arm on her hour-long trek down to the village again. She paused and gave Istvan an eye of caution as he gradually entered the path. Her gaze drifted around, like a person in thought, and she only awkwardly offered him a soft "Good morning" an uncomfortable time later.

Madeline lacked a certain social awareness and a powerful insight into others. This was not a moment of insight, and she obviously did not know what to do. Idly conversation was a definitive weakness for her.

"Good morning. I did not expect many to be awake at this hour," he returned, smiling cordially, conveniently misdirecting her to believe that their meeting on the path had been coincidental.

Noting the book, he gestured absently, "Planning to write some today? If you are going to the library, I can help you with the finer techniques of quill and ink... if you wish."

Madeline looked sceptical but offered him a non-committal shrug. "I... I guess," she replied with the same level of apathy. "Aren't you worried they'll gut you for talking to me? I could be casting an evil spell on you or something," she added, placing heavy sarcasm on the comment about evil casting.

Istvan snorted, rolling his eyes dramatically at the words. He considered the woman for a moment before answering.

"I imagine tongues are already wagging that I am walking with you. Luckily, you are not evil or perhaps I would be more concerned about these spells of yours."

"Good to know," she answered, again in a non-respondent and apathetic way. "At least one of you has an open enough mind to come to that obvious realization."

Istvan smirked slightly. "Honestly, I do not know what to make of you and your companions. The priest seems humble enough and of a good heart.

Your John is somewhat of a hothead and talks in the tone of the Fey, which makes many overly curious. I believe the problem is in your choice of languages. A holy book is written in the language of the Nine Hells? Naturally, it arouses suspicion, and your Priest's arguments were not likely to be sufficient for most to come to an understanding, " he replied at length, stopping to regard her closely, watching her eyes.

"Tell me, Madeline, should I be wary?"

Madeline smirked slightly through Istvan's long and drawn-out speech. "So first you conclude that I'm not evil, so you're safe, but then you ask me to verify that determination?" She gave him a critical tone in her response. "Sounds like I was a little hasty in my assessment," she mumbled through a long sigh.

"Should you be wary? Hell, if I know," she answered finally. "Yeah, Father Antonio is a very humble and very good man. I'd say you hit the nail on the head with that one. And bonus points for John being a loose canon. Unfortunately, I have no idea what you mean by Fey to confirm or refute that observation. If by Fey you mean Irish, then yeah. That's true. He's Irish. I don't know what that has to do with anything, though." Madeline seemed fairly bored with this course of the dialogue.

"There's only one Hell, not nine," she corrected him flatly. "And I have no idea what language they speak down there if any. You should talk to Antonio about that business."

Istvan frowned. Apparently, his sour mood was contagious because Madeline grew more and more difficult with each passing moment. "Perhaps I shall," he answered casually. "In any case, I can read any language if I choose. If you do not mind, I would like to read one of your holy books. In that way, I can attest that your God's teachings are not infernal," he added neutrally, his tone daring yet genuine.

"Any language you choose, eh?" Madeline remarked to herself, clearly finding Istvan to be arrogant, but she didn't comment on it past that.

She continued to walk as she paused in her response. "Let's hypothetically say that you can read Latin," she said in the sort of way that scholars often did when engaging in some intellectual argument (though not one that was charged by emotions). "Because I mean, I can barely read it, but let's say you can read it pretty well. No one else here seems to be able to, except for Anthony and maybe Simon, or else they'd have read the Bible last night to confirm what the three of us were saying about it. So, I have to wonder what your intentions are. If this is a trick, you'll screw me over and tell everyone that it's super evil or something. If you're sincerely curious, what makes you think anyone will believe what you have to say? All the people here seem to believe in magic. What's to stop them from thinking I cast some spell on you or something to make you say that my religion is about love and forgiveness? I mean, it's not like anyone else can verify what it says, right? And it's easier to think I did something nefarious than to accept that I'm not some monster in disguise. Especially after everything that's happened."

Istvan attempted to offer a casual shrug, but it translated into something awkward. "... Why do you find it odd that we should believe in magic?" He inquired, largely thinking out loud. "I would have expected an educated woman such as yourself to be well versed in Arcane Knowledge..."

Madeline stopped and looked at him critically, obviously confused by his genuine curiosity. "... are you... are you serious?" She replied in a gentler voice than he was expecting. "Magic isn't real, Istvan. Magic is something that people invented to compensate for their own lack of understanding of science."

The statement was obviously absurd, but Istvan frowned in confusion, meeting her eyes straight. Her dismissal of magic, albeit ridiculous, was offered gently and with concern for his response; as if she knew it would change his world to hear these words, she offered them with care and respect. "But it is real," Istvan replied, equally bewildered. "It is measurable and quantifiable. I would argue that it is more studied than science... are you... are you a scientist?" He was hesitant but excited at the same time. As an Artificer, his field was a marriage between Arcana and Science, the latter of which was a small and quickly developing field that intrigued him greatly.

Madeline seemed even more confused. "Well... wait, if I say yes are you going to try and burn me at stake?" She offered in a guarded tone. She shook her head slightly. "Look, that doesn't matter. How can you genuinely look me in the eye and honestly tell me that magic is quantifiable? That's... I mean...

What? Magic's not real, Istvan. I mean, how can you quantify something that doesn't exist beyond zero?"

Istvan frowned harder as they continued, turning to look at the ground. He was now extremely confused as Madeline seemed genuine in her dismissal of magic. They stopped when Madeline paused to examine a tree she seemed to recognize and had just put out a few new shoots. She shifted the book in her arms and reached into her pocket, pulling out the metal ring that held a variety of contraptions on it. She sifted through the items until she pulled a pink one out and then, much to Istvan's surprise, pulled a small blade from it and began to cut off small twig-like branches on the aspen, tucking the branches into her pockets as she did.

Istvan forgot all his confusion as his eyes latched onto the strange tool she had just mundanely used. His hand reached out almost of its own accord.

"That knife. How...who created such a work?" he asked softly, his tone clearly one of professional interest and perhaps reverence.

Maddy eyed him carefully, taking the knife off the equally impressive carabeener and closing the blade before handing it to the clearly curious Istvan. She did this without looking at it as if it were second nature. "Surely you have knives, where ever you're from?" She asked, rather curious about Istvan's reaction. This only reinforced that the miraculously crafted knife was a forgettable mundane contraption to the woman.

"This is a pocket knife and not a very good one," she explained. Smiling faintly, she pocketed the rest of the key chain.

Istvan glanced into her eyes, gratitude clear as he accepted the curious tool. His fingers quickly explored, plucking open each tool and examining it with a critical eye.

"Knives? Yes, of course, but the workmanship of this is amazing. Such detail and so small. And they all connect together. This is absolutely inspiring. I don't think even Gnomes and Dwarves could create something like this, let alone the Elf metalsmiths," he ventured, hushed and intrigued.

With some reluctance, he closed the tool back to how he received it and held it out to Maddy.

Madeline's critical look shifted into a bit of a frown. "Gnomes. Right," she said as she accepted the knife.

Madeline did not say anything else as she turned to cut a few more of the new shoots from the aspen and finally pulled out the key chain to return the knife to its home with the other dangles. She started walking again toward the town.

"I'll uh... I'll draw a design sketch of it if you want," she offered hesitantly. "It's not all that hard to make."

Maddy's pace hadn't changed, though she seemed to be examining the aspens as they walked.

The silence gave Istvan's mind a chance to revisit Maddy's insistence that magic wasn't real. "What if... what if I were to prove to you that Magic does indeed exist?" He approached carefully.

Madeline cocked a sceptical but academic eyebrow. "Oh?" She replied, obviously humoring him.

"I believe that there is a communication barrier between the Three and the rest of us," he speculated while nodding at her. "In that vein, I suspect that you know full well the meaning of magic but that perhaps it uses another name in your land. Perhaps the word magic implies foolishness to you, where I mean something other than what you infer?" Madeline stopped and offered Istvan an appraising look. If he had to guess, those expressions were few and far between where she was concerned, and so to earn one was something of a sign of respect. Istvan smiled genuinely in return. "Ok, I'll bite," she replied with the first hint of interest in her tone that he had yet heard.

Istvan smiled again, revealing a row of bright white, perfectly straight teeth. Madeline found herself blushing slightly. Istvan was a very attractive man. "Ah. May I?" He asked, gesturing for Madeline to hand him her book. She did so freely. "Now, I shall make this tome levitate using magic as the appropriate energy source," he explained in an academic tone.

Madeline instantly frowned in hesitation at his announcement of what he was to do, and as Istvan began murmuring the ancient words and the book slowly rose from his hands, the woman gasped in horror and threw her hands over her mouth to keep from screaming.

That was not at all the response he had been looking for.

Madeline's physical posturing suggested one of fear while her eyes were wide and her pupils were dilated. Her breathing had begun to increase rapidly as well.

Her nostrils flared a bit, and her voice quivered as she spoke. "You're one of those... things..." She swallowed hard. "Dear god." She swallowed again and overcame her fear enough for one last statement: "Stay the fuck away from me, got it?" She told him in a gravely serious voice as she promptly turned around to head away from the village and back toward her cabin.

Istvan had no way of knowing that Madeline's first and only exposure to magic was through the demons that destroyed her lands. Suddenly, Albus's advice that he keep his magical abilities quiet seemed to repeat itself in his head. There was more than one reason not to advertise his ability.

It was the second rejection he had felt, and the sun had barely risen past the horizon. Hanging his head in defeat, Istvan trudged his way back to the village, walking into the library and dropping heavily into one of the chairs with a dejected sigh. Albus was already hard at work, finalizing a sketch he had begun the previous day of a bugbear. He looked up and offered Istvan a warm smile as he entered, but his look turned to concern upon seeing his expression.

"What has happened?" He asked, putting down his quill.

"I am an idiot," he explained as if that was all that needed to be said.

"I was walking with Madeline on our way to town and decided to show off. I infused her sketchbook with a simple levitation spell, and she went crazy. Apparently, her people are horrified of magic. It was much like the others reacted to their speaking of Infernal. I am afraid I set any progress back a few centuries."

"I should have listened to you. I have a big mouth," he explained, deflating onto one of the chairs and sighing.

"Horrified of magic?" Albus repeated in awe, his eyes wide. "In what context? As in that, they chose not to believe in magic, or they have never experienced it?" He asked, trying to understand the situation. "Those are two very different things, my friend. Do you have a sense of which?"

Albus didn't even address that Istvan didn't listen to him. It didn't seem to matter to him. The old man's reaction was one of concern and even comradery. It left him with the feeling that Albus was a true friend.

Istvan opened his eyes and sighed, sitting up and shrugging.

"She said I was one of 'them' and to stay away from her. I guess it could be that she meant the demons that seem to have ravaged all of our lands. I am not sure. If that is the case, then I would say they have never seen magic before the invasions."

"You should see her equipment, Albus," he added with wide eyes before he blushed and considered his words. He had not meant her physical equipment.

"She has a device that holds a knife and other utensils all together with such fine details. I don't think I have ever even seen Elf or Gnome work that fine. She even scoffed when I mentioned Gnomes as if she did not believe in them. It is really weird," he finally adds, leaning back and pondering the strangeness.

Albus digested the information with intrigue. "I once visited a land where no magic had existed for many centuries. The Cuthbertians had killed all of the mages in the area, and it was isolated. Over the centuries, people simply forgot about it. In their eyes, no such thing existed, nor was it a part of how they understood the world. I was young then, and I conjured a flower to hand to a pretty girl. I thought it would help her see the truth; that magic did exist."

"To make a rather long story short, I am lucky to have survived the response of the people. In fact, this scar is from my escape. The response was violent and swift, much like the response that the clerics had toward learning that the holy book of the Three is written in infernal, with one difference: It is the look in their eyes. The people of that village had terror in their eyes like nothing I had ever seen. It was all that was there. The clerics last night had a look of hatred in with their fear. Hatred can be appeased with logic. Not eliminated, but abated. Pure fear cannot be."

"It wasn't until I got older that I actually realized my mistake. That flower was not for the pretty girl; it was for me to satisfy my own need to be right rather than to provide that young girl with what she needed to accept the truth." Albus sighed slightly as if regretting the error of his ways and the potential love he lost.

He shook his head slightly. "Tales of times long past. You said that Dr Parker went crazy; tell me:

how did she behave? If it is true that her only exposure to magicks is from the demons, I am surprised that you have no claw marks. It also is an important piece of evidence regarding the state of these strange people. And this tool she has... could you describe it? Draw it, perhaps?"

Madeline had offered to provide Istvan with more than just a drawing, but it seemed unlikely that she would do so now, given her reaction.

Istvan thought back to the encounter and frowned. He had lost more than he had thought.

"She reacted fairly well. She was angry and scared, but she did not threaten violence, simply removing herself from the situation," he recalled, slumping even further into his chair. "Rao would be pleased," he reported dismally. "The hand that stays violence is the hand that builds bridges, or so the saying goes..."

Istvan started to describe the knife and the other contraptions he had seen on her key chain of wonders. "I am sure she will not draw it for me now," he lamented. "Perhaps she would do so for you, though? She seems keen to interact with those of an open mind, and I cannot think of a mind more open than one belonging to Delleb." He offered his friend a weak smile.

Albus was clearly fascinated by the implications. "I am most interested in this contraption that it impressed an Artificer," he replied, stroking his white beard as he thought. "It must be remarkable indeed, and it is interesting that she volunteered to share its design so freely when she has volunteered so little else. Given all of the scrutiny surrounding them, I doubt she would do so if it were of evil orientation."

"As for her response, perhaps there is yet hope. It is a rare person who can temper their fear with logic, but perhaps that is what she has done. Most interesting, most interesting indeed. If she can think rationally even in the presence of great fear, then she will not cling to hatred, my friend," Albus told him gently as if to try and raise his spirits. "I will speak on your behalf as best I can."

"I suppose I ought to travel to their cabin before this confusion can spread," he said, rising from his seat slowly. "Shall I tell her anything on your behalf, or ought I restrain and allow you the opportunity to reconciliation yourself?"

Istvan waved a dismissive hand. "Nay, it would only hinder your efforts. If it becomes a topic, perhaps express my displeasure to have offended her so that it was unintentional, but only if she makes the issue her own."

Albus nodded and gathered his bag, leaving Istvan alone in the library for the piece of real solitude he had experienced upon arrival.

Istvan groaned in stiff pain as he laid down the quill, rubbing his eyes and stretching his shoulders. He had lost track of time and looked down ruefully at the up-to-date volumes of his known infusions.

He doubted that it would be useful to anyone other than him, at least at this stage. If the community did survive, perhaps the children produced would be interested in the rare trade.

Stowing the book on a shelf and the time on the botany of the area, he made his way outside, taking in what was now a mid-afternoon sunshine and watching the new villagers make their way about the village square. Everyone seemed hesitant and yet curious. He wondered when the newness of this new place would wear off. For now, however, it was a welcomed change to the world he had been born, a world utterly savaged by demons.

Only after several minutes of absent people watching did Istvan realize that Albus and Robin were having a rather serious conversation.

"Tell me again," Robin said in a serious and hushed tone. "What exactly happened."

"I went to bring them some of the bread as a peace offering and to see about the holy book. The woman was upset regarding something which had transpired earlier in the morning, but I found her attending to the priest, who had taken to illness. He had not used his prayers to heal himself, and this illness appears to be worsening. The woman had made a tea of aspen shoots and claimed it helped to dull his pain and lower his fever. She refused to give me the book, but the sickly cleric argued on my behalf and begrudgingly gave me what she calls a missal. According to the cleric, it is the book by which the ceremonies are conducted, and it contains all of the quotations of scripture from the holy book, divided into three years worth of weekly services."

Robin paused and frowned. "Why has he not healed himself?" He asked seriously.

"I inquired. He did not know what I was speaking of and answered that he cannot heal."

Robin's eyes widened. "Only neutral or evil clerics cannot heal," the younger man thought out loud. "Speak nothing of this to anyone until we have thoroughly examined this missal of theirs. There is no need to cause any more concern than is needed."

Albus nodded solemnly and clutched the missal tighter. Istvan knew there was no way the man would let anyone damage the book and something told Istvan there was more to the story. Albus offered Istvan a concerned look as he entered the library. "My friend, do you have a moment? There is an urgent matter we must discuss," he said seriously.

"What is wrong, Albus?" Istvan replied, obviously concerned, but stepping out of the way and closing the door to the library as the older man stepped inside.

Albus frowned slightly and pushed the door shut. He shook his head slightly and sighed a little. "I went to speak with the Three, to bring them bread as a guise to make peace. Many issues resulted from this, some of which are of direct interest to you. However, I shall start from the beginning."

"Lady Madeline was indeed quite frightened by your use of magic before her. She was hesitant to open the door for me when I arrived, but she did so, as they apparently needed the bread. I was not at all prepared for the condition of the cleric nor the state of this cabin, which I shall detail for you later. He is quite ill, but I would have assumed he would have prayed to his god to heal him. He had not done this."

"This compounded Lady Madeline's anxiety. She seems to be kind, and she has done a great deal toward tending to the man's injuries. She has concocted a tincture made of aspen shoots to dull his pain and reduce his fever. When I inquired, she claimed that the pulp extracted from the bark has alchemical properties known to her people, something she called Salicylic Acid. It concerned me that she would use Acid to cure when we Arcane know it to be destructive rather than restorative, but this alone is not the whole issue."

"The main of it is this: it is common knowledge that all goodly priests have been blessed with the graces to request healing power. I naturally asked the man why he had not asked for his God's blessing of health. He told me that he and Madeline had prayed for his health, but his answer seemed as though he did not understand my question. I inquired about an instant healing, and he smiled and assured me that such a thing was magic and therefore not real."

"The woman frowned deeply at this, and it was clear that she did not share your experience with the cleric, likely for the better, given their peculiar response. The man continued and thanked me for bringing them the bread. Istvan's illness is quite severe, and I believe he knows this but attempts to hide it from Lady Madeline and John. The gratitude he showed me for a simple loaf of bread... He asked me to apologise for offending the others, so they felt no option but to handle him harshly, and he wishes to seek reconciliation with haste."

"Here in lies the conflict. As an evil man, Istvan would not seek to reconcile with those who so clearly had wronged him. This man wanted to extend forgiveness and was true to the concept! Lady Madeline requested that we leave Antonio to his rest, so I used the opportunity to discuss your shared conflict. Her opinion was this: She does not deny that she cannot explain what you did, and that fact is not what upset her so. Rather, it was the similarity that the demons too used magic and so it caused her mind to jump to a connection."

"It was then that she said something rather enlightened. She told me that "Correlation does not imply causation." It was a remarkably insightful phrase, and it was that manner of thinking that kept her from reacting to you more harshly. It shall be the route toward healing and understanding. She admitted to me that she did not get the idea that you, too, were a demon, which she calls an alien, but that given how oddly we all behave, and yes, she believes us to be the odd ones, she did not know what to think."

Albus cocked his eyebrow as if the next statement caused him humour. "She urged me to be cautious if you are an alien in disguise. Of course, I did not reveal that a wizard is capable of magic and that an Artificer did not stir a deep concern within me." He smiled a bit at Istvan as if the jab was meant to be a point of humour, not an insult.

"I spoke on your behalf, friend. I assured her that you were not of such ilk and that in your lands and perhaps in others too, the gods have seen fit to bless some with an ability that is similar to that which her aliens employed. I parlayed your confusion and disappointment in the result of the conversation as well as your concern for the well-being of The Three. It was then that Madeline grew silent. I could see that she has very little trust for any of us here, the one called John included. She seems to fear him more so than the fear your display elicited. She would not elaborate, so I hope to learn more."

"Thus, I offered to share some of my knowledge with her to gain more of her trust. Tonight, once the sun has set, she has agreed to sit and learn of the stars via the instruction of the night sky. She has asked me to give you this, and I believe it is a form of an apology on her part for her reaction, though I would not expect trust from her if I were you. She has many more drawings begun, Istvan. Perhaps she is some manner of Artificer, though not one of magic, as she is so predisposed. She also asked that I give Robin a message: if there is a doctor, which I take to mean a healer of noble origin, among the people, she is willing to pay whatever price to have them tend to Anthony, including any of her amazing machines."

"I passed this message to Robin as per her request, and I believe the young cleric is at their cabin now. It is a most curious state of things, Istvan. And," the old man raised his eyebrows approvingly, "you certainly did not understate the intricacy of their crafts. I have never seen such a collection of items as I did in that cabin. I scarcely would know how to use the majority, and yet Dr Madeline seemed as though the items were sparse and of poor quality!"

"As for your reconciliation, the Lady has agreed to continue her studies here in the library. It is my understanding that she requires a means of escaping John, though this is merely the assumptions of an old man, not her words. She knows you will be present here on occasion, and I have assured her that you shall not cast your magics before her. If you agree to this, I believe peace has been made. I, too, shall refrain from casting until such a time comes when she is properly acclimated to the art and no longer fears it."

"Now, in the meantime, I shall summon an unseen servant to begin writing the translation of these missals. I sense that there will be no evil found in them. If their cleric is any indication of the faith, it will be rooted deeply in forgiveness."

"This is much information," he admitted. "What thoughts have you?"

"I admit, Albus, this scenario, a world of only goodly folk, is not as I would have thought it would be. There is much that seems to border into the grey area, if not even worse. I do not only speak of the strange languages of the three shunned ones," he told the man, clearly confused by how people were acting towards one another.

"That the priest does not heal himself... that he requires destructive energy to heal... I must say that the notion intrigues and concerns me simultaneously. Perhaps I will inquire of Doctor Parker when she returns to the library. I saw her harvesting the branches but did not think of it then."

"I admit still. I am relieved that Madeline may allow forgiveness for my mistake. This diagram is amazing, and I will begin at one to see if I can fashion one for myself. The work is so finely detailed. I admit it is a daunting task, but now I have a start," he added with a beaming smile. Apparently, the gift from the woman was very well received.

"This world... all the great sages of Flanaess have oft said that the truest battles are not between good and evil, but rather, a battle for chaos or order. This land is good, but some see the manifestation of goodness differently than others. For my part, the community cannot thrive in chaos. Without community, one cannot learn truly and deeply. We humans are not smart enough as individuals. We must pool our knowledge to a collective."

Albus smiled. "Listen to me, an old man telling a lecture," he remarked with a chuckle. "And I lecture a follower of Rao on the tenets of the community! How foolish I must seem. Nevertheless, the sages' wisdom seems to ring true here. Our battle is misfocused at the moment. In truth, it will be one for order, not one for goodness."

He looked at the piece of paper that Madeline had drawn for Istvan. "The riots are rather small," he commented. "Even a gnome cannot craft such small things. And yet, this blade is a small wonder compared to the bracelet she wears. At first, I thought it was jewellery, but it is something far more. Small needle ticks along in a circle, and two other needles move at differing paces. She noted that I took an interest and explained its function. She called it a "watch" and said it intends to keep time. Can you imagine, Istvan?! A machine which measures time so accurately?"

Albus shrugged slightly. "I wish she hadn't torn this page from the book. I shall encourage her to keep all of the drawings as a collection in the future."

Istvan frowned. "How could she be so smart as to create such a technical drawing and yet so resistant to the truth of magic around her?" He contemplated in frustration.

Albus merely chuckled in reply. "Perhaps you could inquire of her yourself. As I said, I have arranged to meet with her this evening to instruct her in Astronomy. You are more than welcome to attend, for it is here that I shall approach the issue of magic after I have found the limit of her intellect." Albus seemed to think a few hours would be sufficient here. "With us, both working in unison, correcting this ignorance should be a facile feat. We shall pity her ignorance if she still refuses, but it shan't limit our learning of her strange devices."

Istvan listened and contemplated Albus's strategy. Something in the corner of his mind told him this plan was about to backfire, but he didn't argue. The truth was, he was far too intrigued about Madeline's technology to abandon the discourse now. Albus's god would be thoroughly pleased by this, he was sure.

"If the knife device she provided is something mundane that she thought nothing of, I am sure her other items are even more amazing. I admit that I would love to be able to study them. If they do not believe in mana, I must find out what powers their artefacts. Perhaps their God empowers them through relics and not through his priests." he offered sagely, trying to regain his former composure and ability to think logically.

"I will come with you to study the stars and see if the woman has a mind. She did not seem dense to me or at least uneducated. Besides, I suspect she may have come to a postulation regarding the state of this place, and I am quite curious to see if she reveals it this eve," he added with a tone of agreement. He very much wished to stay in the older man's good opinion.

After several hours, night had fallen, and Albus alerted Istvan that they ought to leave soon.

By the time they made it out to the field, Madeline was already there, wrapped in a blanket as she sat on the ground with her knees tucked into her chest. Her hair was shorter than most other women there and reminded Istvan of a style that a man in his world might wear. Still, it seemed attractive enough, and she had swept the shoulder-length mass off to one side. She was already staring at the sky, apparently mapping what she saw in a notebook. The poor girl's hand was still covered in ink from using the quill.

Naturally, Istvan avoided thinking of these observations, having already embarrassed himself earlier that morning. Still, he couldn't help but to picture her as he had seen her the night before and the way the moon and stars danced on her skin... he was thankful that his trousers hid his reaction. Albus's reaction was very different and entirely directed at the ink-covered hand. He smiled in the sort of way a teacher does when a young student tries at something mundane and makes mistakes. The smile was for the effort.

She looked over to Albus as he arrived, but she did not offer a smile.

Albus moved over to join her. "Ah, so you wish to learn about the stars," he said in a rather grandiose tone that instantly caused Istvan to drop his head into his hand. It was hauty and patronizing, and the Madeline he had experienced would make Albus the fool for his efforts. "You've requested the best, my dear. I was once the supreme instructor for Astrology. As a younger man, of course."

"Uh... yeah... s-sure..." Madeline answered with a mild frown on her brows. If Istvan had to guess, Maddy was humoring Albus, and judging by her response, this was a rare thing and indicated some level of respect for the man. "I was wondering if you could tell me the names of these constellations, actually," She said, her tone sounding more receptive to the potential for instruction. "I'm from the Northern Hemisphere; these constellations here aren't familiar to me."

The answer caused a mild recoil of surprise out of Albus for various reasons, but his head shifted upward, and he took in the sky, suddenly frowning deeply. "Well, of course, I," he stopped as he saw the sky. "Hmmmm..." Something confused the man, and it caused Madeline's expression to grow critical and pensive.

"Dr. Parker, you say you are from the Northern Hemisphere," he said. "What importance does your country have on the patterns of the stars?" Albus asked curiously.

This caused both of Maddy's eyebrows to raise as if that was not the response she had been expecting. "Oh... uhm... The Northern Hemisphere refers to my geographical location on the planet," she explained respectfully. "But it is important because the view of the stars is different from the top of the planet than it is from the bottom, so... people in the

Southern Hemisphere will have different constellations than the Northern Hemisphere... So... you're probably from the northern hemisphere, then? Since you don't recognize these stars either?"

Albus frowned deeply at this response. He, too, had not been expecting something like what she said. "I... a hemisphere?" He finally asked.

Understanding swept Madeline's face. "Oh." She let out, letting her own realization sink in. "Uhm... I... I uhm... I'll try to explain that later," she stammered as she shuffled through her pages. Madeline found a blank one, ripped it out of the book (causing Albus to wince in intellectual pain), and handed it to Albus. "Could you please draw what your stars are supposed to look like?" She asked rather sweetly. She was genuinely interested in what Albus thought the stars were supposed to look like, but something told Istvan it was more like an equal than a pupil, as Albus had intended. "This time of year, I mean."

Albus's expression changed completely. It was becoming apparent to him that Madeline did not need Astrology instruction from him anyway. His plan was quickly unraveling. Humbled, the older man took his seat on the grass next to her and began sketching the patterns of the constellations while Madeline went back to her own drawings, looking up mildly cautiously at Istvan. The distrust was apparent, but at least she wasn't running away screaming or trying to claw his eyes out.

Istvan was not as surprised as Albus when the woman displayed quite an understanding of Astronomy, more so than most people would have in any case. He had noted a level of education in her speech and manners from before.

Their attention to the stars also drew him there, and he looked up critically, trying to note any familiar patterns. He had not expected to find any and was not disappointed when he didn't. The woman's request for Albus to draw what he was expecting to see did cause him to regard her. Ever since Albus's comment about keen minds learning about the truth that this was not their respective home worlds, Istvan had been curiously pondering how one might accomplish that. John's previous statement suggested that Madeline had done just that using the stars. Only now was he starting to see how she had pieced it together.

"Yes, that is a good idea. If we draw constellations from our homelands, we might be able to draw some conclusions about where our homelands relate to one another. If they do relate at all, that is," he related quietly, worried he would offend the woman again quite by accident.

Madeline watched him with a cocked eyebrow, not taking her eyes off him as she ripped out another page to hand to him. "By all means, draw your own," she replied.

The trio worked quietly for a while until Albus finally announced he was finished.

"Excellent," Madeline muttered dryly, and before the man could say anything else, she handed him a piece of tissue paper with dots all over it. "Lay this over yours. It's the night sky of North America without the constellations drawn. It should be the same for Europe and Asia, give or take in latitude.

You'll probably have to move it around, but you know what to do."

As Albus did this, his frown deepened. "There is no similarity," he muttered, confused. "Did you draw it correctly?" He inquired sincerely.

Madeline didn't answer. "Try these two," she said, handing him what she had been working on. "It's the same thing, but I used the star patterns for the Southern Hemisphere and the sky we see from here on this one." At that, the young woman sighed and stood to meander as she kept her gaze upward. "You should do the same thing, too, Istvan," she advised. "The more data points, the better."

"And what does this tell us?" Albus asked, although both Istvan and Albus already knew the answer.

"That we aren't from the same planet," she said bluntly without turning to look at him. "And neither of us, you and me, I mean, are from this planet, wherever that is. We'll see about Istvan here in a second."

Albus was silent and looking at Madeline with a different sort of expression. Albus had nothing to teach her regarding astronomy, and she had figured out the big secret in an impressively short amount of time.

Istvan did a rudimentary look at the star patterns before smiling. It was true; she had used the stars to determine that this world was something new.

"Well, Albus, I think Doctor Parker has shown she is more than knowledgeable of this subject. I admit I did not think any would uncover this mystery quickly. I... I am impressed, m'Lady," he offered quite genuinely.

"This also would explain the language variances. As I told you before, Albus, I was considering that languages independently developed on different worlds, or even lands in some cases, could be quite different and used for different purposes.", he told his friend with a happy smile, one of the first he had worn in this new world.

Looking at Madeline, he took out his own book and jotted down quick notes.

"If you don't mind my extended presence, miss, could you entertain some basic questions on theology or perhaps ecology? Firstly, this is to dispel the conjectures already reached by...others. Other than the demons...ummm.. aliens, does your culture have any knowledge of demons or devils, monstrous servants of the darker powers and Hells?" he asks curiously, clearly trying his best not to offend her, at least not until he had his answers.

Madeline gave him a skeptical look. "Of... what? Uh... no, no, we don't... I mean the aliens... look, I already gave you the missals," she said hesitantly. "If you want to know about the devil, you should probably talk to Antonio. He's the expert there," she added, apparently finding this statement to take away from her train of thought. In it, however, was an interesting revelation. Madeline referred to devils in a singular sense; the devil. Similarly, she and John often referred to their god as the god. John's hesitation toward accepting a pantheon made much more sense in the context of a single-deity world.

"But... So let me get this straight: Antonio can speak Latin, which, by the way, is a language of knowledge and religion, you nut jobs blow a fuse because you think it's some devil worship thing, and you somehow concluded that we must all be from different worlds?" She asked, obviously not understanding where he made the connection. Of course, she had no idea that Albus had made the discovery the previous day with his scry.

"If anything, the fact that we all speak the same language should send up red flags. I mean, the fact that we all seem to be human is confusing enough if we are all from different planets..."

"What do you mean?" Albus asked, not necessarily following.

"Because isolation breeds uniqueness," she answered as though it were obvious. "Haven't you ever gone to some far-off and excluded place where the people, plants, and stuff are all completely different? What is the probability that eighteen people, ostensibly from multiple different worlds, all happen to be human and all happen to know the exact same languages? I mean, you have to factor in that all of these different worlds had such similar geological developments that all the same conditions resulted in the exact same evolutionary and genetic path development to produce humans, let alone humans that all speak the same language. I mean..." Madeline's expression took on a daunted look. "It's freaking astronomical..."

Albus squinted his eyes as he looked at her. "You speak of mathematics," he ventured, testing the limits of Madeline's knowledge again.

"Well, yeah, I guess, but it's just basic math," Madeline answered casually, obviously not seeing what Albus was asking and deep in thought. An idea seemed to hit her, sending her daunted look into an overwhelming one. "I... I've gotta go..." she muttered as she collected her things.

"Wait, why?!" Albus let out. Madeline had now intrigued him, and he wanted to learn more. "Wait, I must know. What is your knowledge of mathematics? Your machines? I must know of them!"

Madeline paused and gave him a mild look of disbelief at the outburst. "My what? Uhm... look, it would probably take months for me to go over all the ridiculous math, I know, so... I mean, can we do that later? and... I don't know, tell me what machines you're talking about, ok? Ok. I've gotta go."

"But why?" Albus continued, obviously very confused.

"Because if I don't get this idea written down, I'm going to forget it," she said shortly.

"Wait!" Istvan called after her, trotting up to her and motioning to reach out and stop her before second-guessing himself. Out of the corner of her eye, she caught the movement and spun violently around, casting him a look of complete distrust. "Please wait," he added. That she loathed him so strongly bit at his self-esteem. Nothing could injure a Raotian more than the breakdown of the community.

"We... we have a paper here," he offered pleadingly. "And you shan't find better minds than present company. Albus's god rejoices in the sharing of knowledge. If you have stumbled upon an idea... it would be a great honor to him to have it shared."

Madeline continued to give him a look of distrust. Eventually, she broke eye contact long enough to consider Albus before letting out a frustrated sigh and walking back to him. Inside, Istvan was silently rejoicing.

"Ok, listen," she said in her normal all-business tone. "That our stars don't match means one of two things. Either we are from different planets or from the same planet in different timelines."

Albus and Istvan blinked together in confusion.

Madeline rolled her eyes slightly. "It's way too hard to explain right now, so listen. Remember you guys who wanted me to explain all of this? If you think the probability is a challenge, wait until you hear about quantum mechanics. Anyway, it doesn't matter. Honestly, I think the latter is what's going on here. The statistics required to make the multiple-world theory actually valid would require 85 universes worth of elementary particles. Last I checked, uni meant one. String theory, on the other hand, and general relativity, too, allows for multiple timelines to avoid time travel paradoxes and adjust for universe expansion and particle creation. I think it explains black holes too, but who really knows."

"Basically, the universe is nothing but a huge Boolean supercomputer. Anytime any choice could be made, the timeline splits, one for each possibility presented by choice. Simple choices lead to very similar timelines. The more branches you have, the more different the world becomes. This sort of branching isn't limited to the simple human decision-making splits either. Pretty much anything can represent a branch. In some timeline somewhere, there are still Dinosaurs roaming the earth while in another, we fought the aliens with super duper advanced technology and kicked their asses."

Maddy paused here, offering a vindicated grin at the assessment. Somewhere, in her way of viewing... everything... they had won the war, and this knowledge gave her a degree of comfort.

Albus and Istvan continued to blink at her in confusion. "...I..." was the only word Albus managed to get out.

"So... we are from your history?" Istvan stumbled around in his confusion.

Madeline took on a patient expression. "No," she answered, calming down, spilling everything her mind had put together. "No, we are from the same relative time on different timelines. Here," she said, stooping to the ground and tracing what looked like a river delta. "The timelines are like roots or a tree or something. We think time flows linearly, but it's not some straight line. There are lots of paths for a time. We humans can't exist outside of the flow of time, though, so as far as our minds are concerned, we float regularly in a straight line, completely unaware of all of these other branches and the people who float on them." Madeline bisected all of the lines with a horizontal cut. "See this line? It represents the relative "now." If you think about it, you could be sitting on this branch, me on this one, and Albus over there, and we would all cross this line simultaneously. "Now" for each of us is the same, but how we experience it is different because we're on different paths."

A chill went down Istvan's back as he regarded the young noblewoman before him. Oddly, her explanation seemed to make sense.

"So, we're all humans in the actual definition of the word, and we all have similar languages because we must all be from co-located timelines. I wouldn't be at all surprised if there were a strong overlap to some people's star patterns," she added with a grin. Maddy suspected none of them would match hers with any fidelity. "Actually, I also wouldn't be surprised if the aliens attacked us all simultaneously. They had some way to alter how time flowed; it wouldn't be surprising if they figured out how to hop across these lines to accomplish what they did."

Madeline looked up again to see that their confusion was only mildly decreased. "Look, guys, I get that you think this is cool and all..." she offered, trying to back-step her way out of this discussion.

Albus used the opportunity to regain his awareness. "My dear lady, please forgive me," he offered in a quiet and humbled voice. "I came here this night to teach you of the great knowledge and have instead learned that it is I who requires instruction. Our ignorance has tested your patience, and you have been kind to attempt to remedy this. Still, alas... such vast knowledge could scarcely be digested through this one evening, let alone understood. It is amicable... perhaps you could come to the library and instruct us in this knowledge...?"

OTHER BOOKS BY THE AUTHOR

Karmic Love

Undercover

Eternal Love

Undying Lust

The Good Taste

Offence and Justice

A Model for Murder

Lethal Legacy

Lethal Legacy 2

Paranormal Club

Enchanted Souls

Beginners of Nowhere

Wildflower

Mystic Agent

Dark Angel

Lonesome Moonlight

The Eerie Egg

A Romantic Crime

Passionate Alien

Dragon Knight

The Critical Case